THE LONG SHADOW ON THE STAGE

Nichole Heydenburg

The Long Shadow on the Stage
Copyright © 2020 by Nichole Heydenburg
All Rights Reserved

Edited by Alex Noelke
Cover Design by: Stone Ridge Books

ISBN 978-1-7349015-0-4 (eBook)
ISBN 978-1-7349015-1-1 (paperback)

Dedicated to Zed. Thank you for always believing in me, for pushing me to keep trying, and not letting me give up on my dreams. I love you.

THE LONG SHADOW ON THE STAGE

CHAPTER 1:
Jackson

Two weeks until I'm done with *Dispatching David*. The thought was terrifying, but also freeing. Jackson Birkman had been starring as the lead actor, David, on the popular TV series *Dispatching David* for the past five years. It had been great to have a steady income, to not have to worry about paying rent, to be able to live his life the way he wanted to without money holding him back. But that was all about to change. He had blown the majority of his savings on a newer, much larger apartment, one that wasn't on the sketchy side of NYC. He had bought a brand new 2015 BMW 750Li because everyone, including his girlfriend, expected him to get rid of his old junker. And okay, maybe he had purchased several more luxury cars simply because he could. The worst part of the show ending, though, was how disappointed his girlfriend was in him. He had tried his best to save up for a nice engagement ring, but he had other things on his mind besides getting married.

He wasn't in a rush, even though Clara was dropping every kind of hint she could while still maintaining some semblance of her dignity. Clara wanted to move in with him, get married, have kids, and become a wrinkly old married couple together. Jackson thought he would be okay with most of that but wasn't sure about the kids part. He had recently accepted the idea of getting married, mostly because Clara was so great. She was everything he had been looking for: smart, witty as hell, long gorgeous blonde hair, and a perfect body. She did things like bring him lunch when he couldn't leave the set for a break and always bought him groceries when he didn't have time. She was so thoughtful and always looked out for him. She had his best interests in mind, and he loved that about her. He loved everything about her, really. It was only the idea of forever that scared him in the slightest, but he knew once they were married and had a couple of kids and settled down, he would lead a happy enough life. He would be content with the vision Clara had for their future because he wasn't creative or independent enough to consider what he wanted; he was more than willing to let Clara have her dream. Because she loved him. And if you love someone, you only want them to be happy.

***

Jackson leaned over to grab his cell phone from the nightstand next to his bed. It was only 7 a.m. Damn. He didn't have to be at work until noon because they were only shooting one scene today. He figured he might as well get up anyways. It was impossible for him to sleep in most of the time. Besides, if he woke up now, he would have time to eat a decent breakfast and if he was feeling up to it, maybe he could even go over his lines a few more times. Clara was in the shower, so he decided to surprise her with breakfast by the time she got out of the bathroom. She would be in there for a while anyways. Although she didn't technically live with him, she stayed the night often enough that somehow his living room had acquired sequined accent pillows and a teal and white chevron rug, his bathroom cabinets were full of make-up and tampons, there seemed to always be random pieces of glitter scattered around the apartment, and he had lost the space of more than half of his closet from her intruding clothes and shoes. He didn't complain much; he liked having her around. He just wished she would ask how he felt about her decorating choices. It was still his apartment, after all.

Jackson stumbled into the kitchen half-asleep and turned on the coffeemaker. Okay, he had to admit that was one of Clara's belongings he didn't mind having around. It was so convenient because it had an option for a single cup of coffee, instead of brewing an entire pot. He made two cups of coffee and started cracking eggs. He slid a few slices of bread in the toaster and began mixing batter for waffles. Clara would be happy; waffles were her favorite. As he was finishing up cooking breakfast and setting the kitchen table, Clara walked into the kitchen.

"God, that looks great. I thought I smelled waffles." She kissed him lovingly and grabbed the syrup from the fridge. "You're the best."

Jackson grabbed her for another kiss, smiled, and sat down next to her. "I'm glad you think so."

Clara sighed in contentment after taking a bite of a waffle. "How did you sleep? I thought you didn't have to be at work until noon today."

"Yeah, I couldn't sleep any longer."

"Sorry, sweetie. I hope it wasn't because of me," Clara said, looking down at her breakfast and pouting slightly.

God, she looks adorable at all hours of the day, he thought.

"Not at all. I like when you stay the night. I'm just stressed, you know?"

"I know, but you'll find something else. I'm sure plenty of directors will want to hire you now. You've been the lead actor in a hit TV show for the past five years, Jackson! You won't have trouble finding work," Clara responded with a reassuring smile.

It was encouraging how much faith she had in him, but of course she didn't quite understand how the entertainment industry worked. He could find another acting job, but would it be a role he enjoyed? Would it be another popular show, one that people would watch and care about? And would he still be making hundreds of thousands of dollars per episode? He would miss the lifestyle he had grown accustomed to.

I should have been smarter with my money. Why did I ever think it was a good idea to buy so many cars? If things get rough, I can always sell them. But I doubt I'll make enough to recover from the rest of it. My stupid mistakes…

"Jackson? What are you thinking about? You have a weird look on your face," Clara asked, bringing him back to reality.

"Huh? Oh. Just work stuff."

"What about work? Are you okay?"

"I'm fine."

He speared a large chunk of a waffle with his fork and drowned it in syrup, hurriedly changing the subject. He didn't want

Clara to know how worried he was about his financial issues. There was no use in making her worry. "Does everything taste okay?"

"It tastes great. Thanks for making breakfast," she said, smiling and reaching across the table to grab his hand. She laced her fingers through his and gazed into his eyes. "Jackson?"

"Yeah?" He asked, preparing for the worst.

"You want to get married, right?"

Dear God. It's not even 8 and she's already at it!

"Clara, of course I do. Someday."

Clara's demeanor immediately changed. "Someday... It's always someday. We've been together for six years."

"I know how long we've been together, Clara."

She unlaced her fingers from his and folded them on the table. "Are you not ready? Do you not love me? What is it about getting married that terrifies you *so intensely*?"

"You know I love you. That has nothing to do with this."

"What?" She asked, standing up and kicking back her chair. "That has everything to do with this!" She exploded. "If you don't love me, just tell me now before I waste any more of my time."

And all I wanted out of today was to enjoy my waffles and not screw up too badly during rehearsal...

"Calm down. I don't think now is the right time. I mean, with the show ending, money's going to be tight for a while. It would be hard to save for an engagement ring, a wedding, and a honeymoon all at the same time."

"What are you talking about? You're a celebrity actor on an Emmy award-winning TV show-"

"Well, yeah, but..."

"Jackson, what did you do with all of your money?" She asked, folding her arms across her chest and glaring at him accusingly. "You blew it all, didn't you?"

Jackson clenched and unclenched his fists. She was starting to piss him off. It was his money, so why did she care?

"Clara, listen to me. I want to marry you. In a few years, when things are settled down and we don't have to worry as much about money."

"If we keep waiting for you to become a financially responsible adult, then we're never going to get married. Just forget it." Clara stood and walked over to the sink, furiously scrubbing her dishes and letting them clatter loudly into the sink when she was finished.

Jackson came over to her and wrapped his arms around her waist. "I love you." He kissed the back of her neck. "I love you so much, Clara."

He could tell she was fighting back a smile despite her anger, but eventually she gave in and turned to face him. "I love you too."

He smiled. "Then why do you ever doubt me? I want to spend the rest of my life with you. I want to marry you, have a couple adorable little rugrats, buy our dream house, and spend eternity with you wrapped in my arms."

And it was true, for the most part. In that moment, it was exactly what Jackson wanted. He reserved the right to change his mind, but it's not like they had a specific timeframe set.

"Really?"

"Yes," he said, kissing her hand gently.

"Then promise we will get married next year."

Jackson swallowed hard and nodded. "Okay. Next year."

***

"Jackson, *please* just five more minutes?"

"Sorry, I really have to leave. You can stay in the apartment if you want though. I don't think rehearsal will be very long." He kissed Clara on the top of her head and smiled goofily. "I'll see you later!"

He hurriedly gathered up the script, his notes, a pen, and a water bottle, and raced out the door. "Shit, I really am going to be late," he muttered to himself. With the slam of his apartment door, he sprinted down the stairs. The elevator was too slow to be worth it right now. He shoved the front door open and shivered with the encroaching cold.

"Fuck, didn't grab a coat." But it was too late to return upstairs, so instead he hailed a taxi and jumped inside. He could have driven one of his cars, but it was always such a pain to pull out of the parking garage when there was perpetually terrible traffic, so much so that he rarely drove. It was almost pointless for him to own any cars with how little he used them.

The taxi driver turned around to look at him. "Are you Jackson Birkman?" He asked excitedly, with a stupid grin spreading across his chubby cheeks.

"Yup. Listen I need to be at rehearsal in like five minutes. Can you get me there on time?"

"Sorry, it's just such an honor to meet you, sir! I'm a huge fan of your show," the older man continued. "I watch it every Sunday night. My wife isn't really into it. She says it creeps her out, but I just love it. The action, the drama, and *your character*-"

Jackson cut him off, "I'm glad you enjoy it. But, please, I'm going to be late. I don't want to piss off the director."

"Alright, alright, I'll get you there on time. Wouldn't want the star to be late."

"Thank you. And really, I appreciate the kind words."

"Anytime, buddy! Ya think I could get an autograph?"

"Sure, yeah." He whipped out his notebook and scribbled his signature on a sheet of loose-leaf.

"Today's my lucky day!" The taxi driver said, finally turning back around and pulling out onto the road.

"Always happy to meet a fan," Jackson said as a goodbye, when the taxi finally screeched to a stop in front of the building where the TV show was filmed.

"It was so great to meet you, Jackson Birkman! Anytime you need a ride, just gimme a call. I'd be honored." He handed Jackson a business card, which Jackson hastily crumpled into his jeans pocket.

"Thanks again," Jackson yelled back, running to the doors of the building. He was only a few minutes late. Maybe it wouldn't be so bad. He was almost always on time, so it shouldn't matter. Although, they *did* need him before they could start filming...

As soon as he entered the room, he immediately wanted to leave. Gus Carver, the director of *Dispatching David* was absolutely fuming: bright, puffy red face, nostrils flaring, stampeding towards him. His six-foot, muscled body was terrifying in every way humanly possible.

Well shit.

Jackson approached him cautiously, apologizing before Gus

could explode. "I'm sorry I'm late, Gus. Traffic was awful. It took me forever to find a taxi..."

"I don't want to hear any of your shit today, Jackson. You're seven minutes late. We could have almost shot an entire scene by now. You think you're so great, huh? 'I'm Jackson Birkman, the star of the show, let those bitches wait for me to arrive!'" Gus said in a taunting, high-pitched voice.

"I'm sorry. I tried to make it here on time. It won't happen again, I promise."

"Damn right it won't, princess. Get in there and make some magic happen. You sure as hell better make sure the rest of my time isn't wasted today. I can't sit around and wait for your sorry ass to show up."

Augustus Carver, aka Gus, was one of the biggest assholes Jackson had ever known, but the thing about Gus was that he was a complete genius. He had won the "Outstanding Directing for a Drama Series" Emmy three times and was sure to remind everyone constantly. He treated the actors and crew like shit, but everyone put up with his atrocious behavior because they all knew it was probably their best chance of 1) becoming rich and famous and 2) finding a job again. Working with Augustus Carver was stressful, yes, but rewarding enough to be worth it. If you didn't mind getting shoved around and taken advantage of at every opportunity Gus seized (which were many), then it all worked out okay.

"What are you doing just standing around? I said get in there! My time is precious, princess."

Jackson hurried into the TV studio and stood near the other actors, who all turned to glare at him, except one thin man who had dark brown hair to his chin, dark brown eyes which were partially obscured by glasses, and dimples. His name was Edgar Peterson. Edgar's parents were both writers and huge Edgar Allen Poe fans, so they had chosen to forever prove their obsession to the world the day they named their son. Edgar had been Jackson's closest friend for as long as he could remember. Their dads had worked together for a while when Edgar's dad was in between writing jobs, so Edgar and Jackson had been thrown together and forced to have "play dates" as small children. Fortunately, it had worked out in their favor because they had stayed close throughout the years and had both decided to try their hand at acting. Jackson had become much more successful but had gotten Edgar a role on *Dispatching David* during season three.

"Jackson, why are you late?" Edgar asked, elbowing Jackson in the side. "Gus has been flipping out."

"I know, I know. I woke up late today."

"Better not let it happen again. People are going to start thinking you don't take your job seriously," Edgar said with a smirk.

Gus was vehemently staring at them. "Are you two done gossiping or can we start the damn scene?"

Edgar immediately spoke up. "I'm so sorry, Gus! We were just discussing-"

"I DON'T CARE WHAT YOU WERE DISCUSSING. You can discuss whatever the hell you want on your own time. Jackson, go over there!" Gus pointed. "Edgar, stand there!"

Gus continued to bark out directions for several moments until he seemed reasonably satisfied. He nodded in appreciation. "Yeah, okay. Good enough."

Jackson stepped into place and spun wildly around. "Kevin, you don't know what you're doing!" He exploded at Edgar's character. "I didn't mean to hurt you. It's not too late to work things out. What do you want? Money? Take it," he begged, pulling his wallet out of his pocket and hastily opening it to flip through the fake bills. He handed a stack of money to Kevin. "If the money's not enough, I'll give you whatever. Anything you want. Just please don't..."

Kevin sprung forward until he was in Jackson's character, David's face. "I don't want your money, David. You never think about anyone but yourself. You act like if you screw up, there aren't any consequences. Well, in the real world, every action has a consequence. I've been waiting a long time for you to get what you deserved, but it appears that God's playing some kind of sick joke on me..."

Gus suddenly stood and walked to the middle of the room, where they were shooting the scene. "What was that?"

"What?" Jackson and Edgar asked simultaneously, both equally terrified their performances hadn't been adequate.

"That was *awful*. Start from the beginning."

Jackson and Edgar both walked back to their original places and pulled themselves back into the scene. Kevin was angry with David because David had slept with Kevin's wife. David's character was notorious for being the worst kind of jerk, but since Jackson was so ruggedly handsome, his character appeared more charming than anything else, making millions of people across the world fall in love with him.

After the scene was finally shot, Jackson, Edgar, and the entire cast and crew were completely drained. Gus had a way of sucking the life out of even the happiest, most carefree people. Besides, he had made them run the scene at least a dozen times and rehearsal had only been scheduled for a few hours. It was now after six and Jackson knew Clara would be upset that he wasn't home yet. She was probably freaking out about him not being home in time for dinner. Maybe he would pick up some flowers for her as an apology. She was obsessed with hydrangeas, so that would make her happy if he surprised her with a bouquet. And maybe he would pick up dinner from her favorite Mexican restaurant.

Once Jackson was home, he discovered Clara wasn't there. He put the hydrangeas and take-out containers from the Mexican restaurant in the kitchen. A note sat coolly on the kitchen counter, in Clara's barely legible handwriting.

Jackson,

I don't know if I can do this anymore. You promised you would be home in a few hours and God only knows what you've been doing this whole time. I'm going to stay at my apartment for a few days and think about things. Maybe you're right; we don't need to get married. It's clearly not what you want, and I'm done trying to force this to work if you aren't going to put in any effort.

Clara

Jackson blankly stared at the page and read it again, the second time Clara's writing scrambled in front of him, the letters blurring together into nonsense, moving of their own accord on the creamy white paper, rising into the air and floating off, past him and out the window, taunting him until he couldn't handle it anymore. He ripped the note off the counter and tore it into shredded pieces.

Jackson slumped onto the cool kitchen tiles and sat with his back against the counter. After a few minutes of feeling sorry for himself, he decided he had to act. It didn't make sense that Clara would leave him because he had gotten home from work late. That had happened before and she had been upset, but never angry enough to break up with him. There had to be something else bothering her. He walked into the living room and sat on the couch, tossing her stupid sequin pillows on the ground, and staring blankly, uncomprehending, at the TV screen for hours. So much for swinging into action. Life was easier this way, if you just let things happen to you as they came. It was much simpler to refrain from trying to stop the inevitable. Jackson always fought as hard as he could for the things he wanted. Perhaps he had been doing it wrong this whole time. Maybe he just needed to lie down and accept that Clara was gone, he was losing his job soon, and things were only going to get worse if he kept fighting against it.

The Long Shadow on the Stage

CHAPTER 2: Jackson

Almost a week later, Jackson woke up frantically in the middle of the night. He reached out to Clara's side of the bed, only to come up empty-handed. He sighed and rolled back over, knowing his sadness was futile, knowing he *had* to do something, and couldn't follow through with letting her leave him. Why did he keep screwing up so badly?

He jumped out of bed, throwing on his wrinkled clothes from the day before. He only took a few minutes to comb his hair and spritz on body spray before bounding out of his apartment and into the chilly NYC November air. Damn. Why did he keep forgetting his coat? He was really on top of things lately.

It would be impossible to catch a taxi at this time of night. Besides, he had three extravagant luxury cars at his disposal. He might as well use them before he was bankrupt and forced to sell them. His 2015 Ford Focus was the most practical of his cars, the least expensive and flashy, but he chose to drive it tonight. He whipped out of the parking garage (which he paid an astronomical monthly fee for) and headed towards Clara's much smaller, much less nice apartment. He had a key, so it wasn't a problem getting inside. He opened the door and crept into her bedroom, finally dawning on the realization that he might terrify her, bursting into her apartment at this time of night. Jackson knew Clara would be asleep because she had endured a long week of meetings for the women's magazine she worked for as an editor. But when he knocked softly on her bedroom door, Clara answered, wearing one of his old t-shirts, her hair a frizzy mess from laying on it. She still looked adorable and he longed to hold her and tell her everything would be alright. He could promise that now because finally he knew what he wanted.

"Jackson," Clara said softly, throwing herself into his arms and sighing in contentment as he embraced her.

"Clara," he replied simply, holding her tightly as he had imagined. "I missed you so much. I couldn't bear the thought of being away from you. I'm sorry I'm not always around and that I'm not as romantic as you want me to be sometimes. I'm sorry I don't consistently do things that show how much I care about you and appreciate you. But I love you more than I have ever loved anyone or anything. More than my acting career, my friends, my cars. You mean more to me than all of it and I know I won't ever be happy unless I can call you my wife."

Jackson got down on one knee and grabbed Clara's hands. "Clara, will you marry me?" Before she could answer, he quickly said, "Uh, I don't have a ring, but we can go pick one out tomorrow, okay? Whichever one you want."

"Oh, Jackson! I love you! Yes, yes, I'll marry you!" Tears streamed down her face as she bent down to kiss him. "Are we really going to look at engagement rings tomorrow?"

"Of course," Jackson said, kissing her again. "Anything you want."

"Will you stay the night?" She asked, tugging on the collar of his shirt coyly.

"Yes. You know, the night you left that note... I brought hydrangeas and Mexican food home for you. I was going to apologize and make it up to you. I'm really sorry. Gus was being a complete dick at rehearsal, and he wouldn't let us leave. I tried to get away."

"You did?" Her face fell. "I'm sorry too. That was so sweet of you. I- I don't know what I was thinking. I didn't want things to continue the way they have been."

"I understand. Next time I'll text you when I have to work late. And don't ever think that I don't want to spend time with you. I wish I didn't have to work so much, but it's not as if I enjoy being away from you."

"Okay," Clara replied, smiling up at him.

Jackson smiled back. His life was starting to feel at peace again. Things would go back to normal now. No more stupid disagreements with Clara, or refusing to finally commit to her, and best of all, soon he wouldn't have to deal with Gus anymore.

"You can move into my apartment too," he blurted out. It made sense if they were going to be married soon. They might as well start moving her stuff in now. She had so much shit it would take forever anyways.

"Oh, I'm so excited! It will be much easier to not have to carry my stuff back and forth all the time. But, Jackson, do you think we can re-decorate your apartment? No offense, but it's not really my style."

"It's not my apartment anymore. It's ours. And we will see about the decorating. One thing at a time," Jackson responded, laughing weakly.

"Fine. Since we're already up, do you want to watch a movie? There's this new Christian Bale one I saw on Netflix the other day. I was waiting to watch it so we could see it together. You like Christian Bale, right?" Clara stared at him adoringly, her brown eyes sparkling in an irresistible way.

Jackson knew he had just sentenced himself to a lifetime of watching Clara fawn over Christian Bale or Johnny Depp, or whatever other male celebrities she found attractive, and he knew that also entailed watching chick flicks and musicals and whatever else she wanted. But it wasn't the end of the world. That was the least of what he would have to deal with for the rest of his life and knowing that made him happy to oblige her wishes and watch the stupid movie.

Since they had stayed up all night, Jackson suggested they go out for breakfast. He let Clara choose her favorite breakfast place because for some reason she never failed to get sick of the weak coffee and flavorless hash browns they served. Slowly, day by day, he would make it up to her. He would prove himself worthy of being her husband, and they would live happily ever after, just like in that movie Clara had convinced him to watch that one time.

***

Jackson knew he had made the right decision, even if Edgar thought he was crazy, even if his parents didn't approve because they thought Clara was after his money, even if everyone else in the world thought marrying Clara was an awful idea. However, there was also the matter of her co-worker *Blaine*. Blaine was 30 and had blonde wavy hair just past his chin, the sort of blue eyes that were the precise color of ocean water and the sky on a perfect clear summer day, and glasses that suited him well. Blaine had been working for the women's magazine a few years longer than Clara, so he had seniority and was technically her supervisor, although he never held that over her. He had been the one to train her and help her adjust when she first started the job. Blaine shamelessly flirted with her and it was no secret to everyone in the office that he was in love with her.

But of course, none of this mattered because Clara was with Jackson. Blaine was content enough being her friend, happy to be close to her in any capacity he could. Clara had never hung out with Blaine outside of work and Jackson knew she would never cheat on him. In fact, Jackson knew he really had nothing to worry about. But the thought of another man being in love with his girlfriend sometimes made him a little crazy. He hated to admit it, but he was jealous. He didn't entirely understand Clara and Blaine's friendship, but he understood why Blaine loved Clara. Despite the disagreements Jackson had with Clara, the way she expected so much out of him, and how half the time she drove him insane with her desire to control every aspect of his life... he still loved her. They were always honest with each other, although sometimes to a fault. Clara expected a lot out of him because she knew he was capable of greatness; she had always pushed him and his success in the entertainment industry could largely be claimed to be her doing. And Jackson knew Clara only wanted what was best for him. So, yes, maybe the spur of the moment proposal hadn't been planned and thought out for months in advance, or hadn't even been the most romantic of proposals, but they were just two imperfect people who loved each other, and isn't that the best anyone can hope for?

***

Jackson strutted into rehearsal feeling the best he had in weeks. Edgar was being weird lately, but he went through phases every once in a while where he was more standoffish and unapproachable than usual. Jackson was used to it after years of being friends with him; he knew it was best to let it pass and act as cordially as possible to him. It was rare that something was wrong; Edgar had a flair for drama and thrived on conflict. One time, when they were seven or eight, Edgar had run home screaming to his parents that Jackson was being mean to him. He claimed Jackson had punched him in the stomach and that he felt like he couldn't breathe. He was screaming and crying his skinny little head off until his face was red and covered in snot. He was upset that Jackson told him he couldn't play with his Tyrannosaurus Rex toy. It was Jackson's favorite and Edgar was mad that he couldn't play with it. That was the first of many times that Jackson had to figure out how to handle Edgar's temper. But Edgar was a loyal friend and he was always there for Jackson. Although, he didn't like Clara, which would be more of an issue once they were married.

Of course, Edgar claimed to like her and had never said otherwise, but Jackson knew him well enough to know when he was lying. It was like the dinosaur toy all over again. Edgar wanted to be the only important person in Jackson's life; there wasn't room for anyone else.

It was the first time they were rehearsing the final scene of the TV show. They didn't shoot the scenes in order, so they still had other scenes to work on, but Gus wanted the last part to be perfect because it was what every loyal viewer would remember for years to come.

"No, no, no!" Gus screamed, standing up from his director's chair and kicking it away for the tenth time that day. He did this so often that the cast and crew weren't shocked anymore. "You're doing it wrong. Didn't you go to school for this shit you call acting? Did you pay attention at all in those fucking classes? Show some *emotion*. Make me feel sorry that you're about to get your tiny brain blown out." He stood still, observing the set for a moment. "Is someone going to pick up my damn chair or do I have to do everything around here?!"

A crew member scuttled over nervously, picking up the chair and placing it upright again.

"Start the scene, princess!"

The gun was aimed directly at Jackson's head.

"Don't do it," he pleaded, this time with tears streaming down his face. "Please. I can fix this. You-you're my best friend. You mean more to me than anyone..."

And with that, Edgar pulled the trigger on the prop gun. Jackson's eyes went wild. He fell backwards onto the stage.

Edgar's character coolly observed the scene, slowly inching forward to look over Jackson's character's now lifeless body.

"Guns are a beautiful thing," Edgar said. "They kill in such a messy way that they sometimes go unappreciated. They seem simple, but it's still an art form, no matter how you look at it. Although the bodies are always awful to take care of, the gun must be checked for fingerprints, and a multitude of things could go wrong…" He paused. "Ah, but if it goes right…then you just might witness the most magical thing you've ever seen or ever will see. It's an experience only a chosen few get to enjoy. But us lucky ones know how breathtaking it is to experience death firsthand. To know that you were the one to snuff out a light, to pluck a soul from this world. I feel…like a god."

Gus came over wide-eyed and smiling and clapped Edgar hard on the back. "Good job, princess. You were kind of creeping me out for a second there. It sounded…believable. Jackson, keep trying. You haven't impressed me yet."

Edgar turned to Jackson and said in a sympathetic tone, "Don't worry, Jackson. You'll get there eventually."

CHAPTER 3: Jackson

Jackson, do you think you could help me with this box? I thought I could get it, but it's heavier than I thought," Clara said, exhaling loudly, her arms shaking while struggling to hold a particularly large box she was trying to carry into his apartment.

"Ah, sweetie! Why didn't you wait for me?" Jackson ran over to her and grabbed the box from her arms. It wasn't that heavy. He brought it into the apartment with Clara trailing after him emptyhanded. "How many do you have left?"

"A lot. Help me," she pleaded, throwing herself onto his black leather couch and curling up her legs to lie down.

"Are you going to bring in anything else?" He asked, frustrated. He didn't mind helping, but if she was going to lay around and not do anything, he at least wanted to know the truth and not have her pretend she was working hard.

"Yeah. Just give me a minute. I'm tired." Clara yawned,

pulling the blanket he always kept on the couch over her body and snuggling into the cool leather.

She didn't look like she was budging an inch, so Jackson grumbled to himself and went back outside to her car, grabbing whatever he could carry to finish moving her stuff in as quickly as possible. He brought inside box after box after box. He stopped beside Clara's car and leaned against it to rest his tired muscles. Jackson heard footsteps rapidly approaching and was about to turn around when suddenly everything went black.

***

Jackson awoke lying in complete darkness. The kind of darkness that was suffocating. Darkness that could drive a person to insanity. It felt like the edges of the...room...were closing in on him. He searched wildly for his phone, a light switch, anything to identify where he was. *What the hell happened? I remember helping Clara move her stuff into my apartment. I don't remember if we finished or not though... God, what time is it? My head is fucking killing me. How long have I been knocked out? And what's that noise?*

He tried sitting up and smacked his head against something, worsening his headache and possibly resulting in a concussion. He reached out to feel around and discovered the most horrifying thing so far: he was trapped in an enclosed space. The walls only extended several feet on either side. With this newfound information, he reevaluated the situation. Okay, he was in a small, enclosed space. Was he trapped in a box or a coffin? Was he buried alive? He touched the floor, which felt like it was lined in rough felt. He touched the walls again, realizing the ceiling was curved.

He listened harder in the darkness, trying to determine where he was. The strange noise now sounded familiar, like a car driving on the highway. *What happened?* He wondered, feeling dizzy and touching his sore head, while trying to clear his foggy mind enough to figure out how to escape. *Okay. I'm in the trunk of a car. How do I get out?* Jackson thought he could remember something about how in newer cars there was a way to escape from a trunk if you were locked inside. He felt around near what he thought was the front of the trunk. Yes! There was a latch! He pulled it and lifted.

The driver spotted the trunk as it flew up and a voice came from the front of the car. "Shit!"

Jackson didn't waste any time, jumping out of a moving vehicle going God only knows how fast on a highway. He rolled onto the shoulder of the road, trying to land towards the grass. It didn't work out quite as planned, but he wasn't dead. Yet. He forced himself to get up, fought past his immense pain, and stood. He half-sprinted, half-limped down the side of the highway, although his left knee felt damaged and he had landed awkwardly on his left shoulder, he knew he had to keep moving. He flailed his arms wildly, trying to flag down a car. "HELP! HELP ME!" He screamed. "SOMEONE IS TRYING TO KILL ME!"

The car he had been trapped in screeched to a halt in the middle of the highway, causing several other cars to slam on their brakes and stop also. A minivan pulled up next to him and the driver, a large man in his mid to late forties who had a wonderful mustache, jumped out of the car.

"Are you okay?" Mustache Man asked.

"That car up there..." Jackson said, out of breath, and wincing from his injuries. "I woke up trapped in the trunk. I don't know who the driver is, but they kidnapped me. We need to find out who they are!"

"Whoa, whoa. Calm down, buddy. We'll get this figured out. I'll call the police."

Suddenly the mystery car Jackson's kidnapper was driving veered into the left lane, nearly causing a head-on collision. Mustache Man whipped out his cellphone and snapped a picture. The car jumped across the median and sped off in the opposite direction they had originally been heading.

"Did you get the license plate?" Jackson asked in a panic.

"Yep." Mustache Man showed the picture to Jackson, zooming in on it so he could see it more clearly.

Jackson bent closely and looked at the license plate number in the picture for a minute before saying, "That's my car."

***

Jackson was at the police station with Mustache Man, who turned out to be named Jerry. He was a mellow, kind man who had been greatly calming to Jackson for the past few hours. They sat in the waiting area, where a coffee pot boiled away, the smell of fresh grounds permeating the stink of criminals that seemed to have permanently taken root in the police station. One of the police officers, who was a woman with bright red, curly hair and a thin frame, came over to the two men.

"Jackson, are you sure you don't want us to call an ambulance? Or I could personally escort you to the hospital? I noticed you leaning heavily on your right leg. You may have broken some bones in your left leg. You appear to have dislocated your left shoulder and the entire left side of your body looks bruised pretty badly."

"Look, I appreciate the concern, Officer, but I promise I'm fine," Jackson said, wincing as he attempted standing to prove he was okay.

"Alright. I can't force you to seek medical treatment, but I would strongly advise seeing a doctor. I'm sure you will want painkillers for your leg. Anyways, we found your car, sir," she said in a crisp voice. "It was abandoned about a mile away from the last location you saw it. We are going to test it for fingerprints later today. We will figure out who stole your car, sir. There's nothing to worry about."

Jerry put a comforting hand on Jackson's shoulder. "Ma'am, I beg to differ. Jackson was knocked out, shoved into the trunk of his own BMW while unconscious, and had to escape from a moving vehicle. Someone wants to harm him, and I don't think this situation should be taken lightly."

Jackson smiled weakly and finally spoke up. He didn't feel like himself at all. His mind was churning slowly, trying to work through the fogginess of the whole day. "I think I just want to go home and rest now, if that's okay. I'm tired and a little beaten up, but I'll be fine."

The police officer nodded. "Alright then. We will give you a call when we know more about the situation. In the meantime, I think it's best if I drive you home and I'll have a rotating staff of police officers watching your apartment. No one will enter or exit the building without our knowledge. Your safety is, of course, our priority."

Jerry raised an eyebrow at Officer Wilson's promise to stake out Jackson's building. "Is that normal police procedure?"

Officer Wilson smiled slightly. "No, not really. The Police Chief is a huge fan of *Dispatching David*.

Jerry chuckled and shook his head.

"Thank you for all of your help," Jackson said to Officer Wilson. He turned to Jerry. "And thank you, Jerry, for being kind enough to stop and help a stranger in need. I appreciate it."

"Anytime, buddy," Jerry said with a smile. "Here's my number if you ever need it. I know a thing or two about cases like this." He handed Jackson a business card, which said Jerry Walden, Private Detective.

"I might just take you up on that," Jackson replied.

"Alright, alright. Let's get you home." The policewoman extended a hand to help Jackson up and he leaned on her to walk to the car. "Are you sure you don't want to go to the hospital first?" She asked, appraising him to determine how bad his injuries were. "You might have broken your left leg and-"

"No. I would really like to go back to my apartment. I'm sure Clara's worried out of her mind."

"Your wife?"

"Girlfriend. Uh, I mean, fiancée. We just got engaged."

"Well, congrats," she said, helping him into her police car. "I'm sure she'll be happy to see you're safe."

Once they arrived at Jackson's apartment, Clara burst out of the double front doors of the building immediately, as if she had been watching from the window, running towards Jackson and nearly knocking him over with the force of her hug.

"Jackson! I was so worried! I tried calling your cellphone a dozen times. I went outside to see if you had taken one of your cars for a drive or something. The BMW was gone, and I found your phone on the sidewalk right here," she said, pointing to a spot a few feet away. "What happened?! Where were you?" She stared at the red-headed, female police officer, noticing her for the first time. "Who is this?" Clara asked in a cooler tone.

"I'm Officer Wilson. Delia Wilson. Nice to meet you," Officer Wilson said, extending a hand to shake.

Clara obliged with a weak handshake. "I'm Clara, Jackson's fiancée." She wrapped her arms around Jackson again and squeezed him, while Jackson tried not to wince. "What's wrong, sweetie?" She asked with genuine concern. "Are you hurt? Oh my God, someone please tell me what happened!"

Jackson looked at Officer Wilson and sighed. Officer Wilson hid a smile with her hand. Now she understood what Jackson meant about his fiancée being worried out of her mind. Clara's personality was the opposite of Officer Wilson's calm, collected demeanor.

"Jackson was knocked unconscious while standing in front of his apartment building. The last thing he remembers is moving your belongings into his apartment. He woke up in the trunk of a car and luckily managed to escape without any major injuries."

Clara sobbed loudly.

Officer Wilson looked alarmed. "But...he's okay. There's no reason to be upset. We are going to have 24-hour surveillance on the apartment building. No one will go in or out without me or one of the other police officers on duty knowing about it." She awkwardly patted Clara on the shoulder. "Anyways, the car that he woke up in turned out to be the BMW you mentioned a few minutes ago. Apparently, whoever kidnapped Jackson also stole his car. They abandoned it soon after Jackson escaped and we are testing it for fingerprints later, so we should be able to find out who the criminal is soon enough." She turned to Jackson. "Is there anyone else who has been in your car so we can rule out people when we test it for fingerprints?"

"Hmm, well Clara, of course. Oh, and Edgar. He's my best friend. I don't think anyone else has been in the BMW…"

Clara nodded in agreement. "Yeah. Just us and Edgar, definitely."

"Alright. In the meantime, stay inside and rest. The important thing is that you're safe," Officer Wilson said to Jackson.

"*Are* you okay, Jackson?" Clara asked softly, still gently sobbing.

He nodded and swallowed hard. "I just want to lie down. And… I could use some painkillers. Help me inside?"

He started to hobble away with Clara's support, which made Officer Wilson chuckle to herself because Clara was so tiny there was no way she was helping.

"I'll be out here," Officer Wilson called out as they left. "I'll let you know if anything happens."

"Thank you," Clara responded for Jackson. "Thank you for bringing him home."

"Just doing my duty," Officer Wilson said with a relieved smile, opening her car door and settling in for the night.

Once Clara and Jackson were inside their apartment, Clara

helped him into bed and gave him the strongest painkillers she could find.

"Are you hungry? Do you want something to drink?"

"I don't think I should mix alcohol with painkillers," Jackson joked.

Clara rolled her eyes and sat next to him on the bed. "Funny. I'll be in the sitting room. Let me know if you need anything, okay?"

Jackson nodded and closed his eyes. He felt completely drained. Everything would seem better after he had a good night of sleep.

"Jackson?" She said softly, not wanting to disturb him, but also having the desire to say something else after all the craziness of the day. "I'm really glad you're home. I don't know what I would do without you." A tear trickled down her cheek and she hastily brushed it away. "I didn't know what to think. I was *so worried*... I don't ever want to lose you." More tears fell as she tried to speak past the ache in her throat.

Jackson was already drifting off and barely heard Clara's words.

"Well, get some rest," she said, kissing him on the top of his head and wandering into the sitting room.

She sat on the couch, mindlessly watching reality show after reality show. The only thing that she could think about was what she would have done if something worse had happened to Jackson. If he had been killed. Who would want to hurt him? A crazed, obsessed fan? Did he have an enemy? It wasn't until the early hours of the morning that she finally climbed into bed to join him, but she couldn't sleep. Jackson tossed and turned all night, crying out in his sleep, and Clara didn't want to wake him. Instead, she lay awake listening to his tortured pleas for help, wondering if he was going to be permanently traumatized from the kidnapping. Would their life together ever be normal? Maybe it was good that his show would be over soon. Maybe everything would be okay afterwards.

Clara decided to let Jackson sleep in, even though she knew he had rehearsal today. He needed the rest. She went into the bathroom to take a shower and felt despaired at the dark circles under her eyes. She started making breakfast and Jackson finally stumbled out of their bedroom after 10 a.m. It was the latest she could ever remember him sleeping in since she had known him. He kissed her and held her tightly for a moment.

"What time is it?" He asked, still half-asleep, fumbling to turn on the coffeemaker and find his favorite coffee mug, a 20-ounce mug from their trip to Asheville last spring. They collected coffee mugs from everywhere they travelled and had a kitchen cabinet overflowing with them.

"It's 10, sweetie."

Jackson's eyes widened and he hastily stumbled back to the bedroom to search for clean clothes he could throw on, but Clara stopped him.

"You don't need to go to work today. I took care of it," she said calmly, knowing she would have to convince him to stay.

"Clara, that wasn't your decision. Gus is going to lose it."

"Actually, he's not. I called him this morning and explained what happened yesterday. He wished you a speedy recovery."

"But how are they going to shoot anything without me there?"

He asked with a helpless look at her.

"I don't know. Don't worry about it. They can't replace you. You're one of a kind," Clara said, kissing him fiercely.

Jackson sighed exasperatedly and sat down on a stool in front of the kitchen counter, while Clara continued to make breakfast. "Fine. I won't go in today. But I'm not happy about this."

"Okay, Mr. Grumpy Pants," Clara teased with a lilting laugh.

Jackson couldn't help but laugh also. Sometimes Clara was so childish, but he needed that lightness in his life. She was bright when all that remained was not.

CHAPTER 4

There he is. The extraordinary Jackson Birkman. I exhaled slowly, cautiously inching forward. Jackson was leaning against a car. I was close enough to Jackson to see that his face was red and his gray long-sleeved t-shirt was soaked with sweat. There were a few boxes placed haphazardly in the back of the car. I moved forward a few more steps, adjusting the gloves on my hands and tightening the hood around my face so no one could make out my features if anyone happened to witness something. I watched Jackson resting against the car for a moment. Suddenly I couldn't take it any longer and rushed forward, hitting Jackson on the back of his head hard enough to knock him unconscious.

I grabbed Jackson under his armpits and dragged him to a car I had waiting in front of the apartment building. I popped open the trunk and looked around, surveying my surroundings. I hoisted Jackson into the trunk of the car, folding in his arms and legs to make sure he was completely inside the trunk, and slammed the door shut. I quickly ran around the car to the driver's side, jumping in. I started the car without putting my seatbelt on and smiled. This was too easy.

I heard footsteps. Someone was coming.

"Jackson?" A female voice called out.

Shit! I pressed my foot down on the gas pedal and accelerated quickly.

I don't think anyone saw me. No. I'm fine. I'm getting away with this. No one can stop me.

CHAPTER 5:
Jackson

Jackson had been spending most of his time in bed, trying to recover from his brief but traumatizing kidnapping. He had never felt unsafe in NYC before, but now he was terrified at the thought of someone roaming the city with the intent to kill him on their mind. As a celebrity with a face most people would recognize, Jackson Birkman thought rather highly of himself. He never considered that being famous would result in anyone wanting to harm him. Of course, he knew there were people who were jealous of his fame, his money, his looks, his acting career… but why did that have to mean those same people wanted him dead? Clearly, he hadn't imagined the possibility of a psychotic fan attempting to murder him.

The thing that he kept turning over in his mind though was how poorly the kidnapping had been planned. Why had the mysterious person chosen to steal one of his cars? Why had he been stowed away in the trunk, when there was an emergency latch that could be pulled to escape? Hadn't the kidnapper researched or inspected the car beforehand? They could have restrained him with rope or handcuffs or forced him to remain unconscious longer with a drug like chloroform or Rohypnol. But most importantly, why had they done it? How could someone have such a malicious intent towards him?

As he contemplated the incident, there was a loud, strong knock on the apartment door. Jackson tried to sit up at a normal speed and winced, realizing he wasn't completely healed yet. At a much slower pace, he pulled himself weakly out of bed and limped to the door, resisting the urge to cry out with every step. He finally opened the door and leaned heavily on the door frame, panting, and trying to stay upright.

"Whoa there. Let me help you over to the couch, buddy," Private Detective Jerry Walden said in a concerned tone.

"I'm fine," Jackson replied, attempting to walk into the family room by himself and nearly collapsing.

Jerry ran over to assist him and they sat on opposite ends of the couch. "So, I guess you're not doing much better, huh?"

"I thought I was okay, until just now," Jackson said with a forced smile.

"Did you ever see a doctor and have painkillers prescribed? Do you want me to grab some for you?"

"Yeah, Clara made me go to the doctor. I think the painkillers are on the kitchen counter," Jackson responded.

Jerry returned a minute later with Jackson's prescription and a glass of water, then waited as he swallowed the pills and chugged most of the water.

"Thanks," he said, adjusting his position on the couch in a futile attempt to get comfortable.

"I thought I would drop by and check on you, since I haven't heard from you."

"Mhm," Jackson said cautiously, knowing Jerry had an ulterior motive.

"Well, and I was wondering if the police had any leads in the investigation. I mean, you were knocked unconscious in the middle of the day. Weren't there any witnesses? A neighbor or someone passing by the apartment complex?"

"The police haven't contacted me, so I have no idea if they have discovered anything new. I doubt it because it's taking them so long to wipe my car for prints."

"The process can take a while. I'm sure they are trying their best. They will want to rule out all of the suspects." Jerry stroked his beard contemplatively. "You don't think it was that fiancée of yours, do you?"

"Clara? No, that isn't even a possibility."

"You were helping her move her belongings into your apartment when the incident occurred, correct?"

"Yes…"

"Was she inside the apartment when you were knocked unconscious? Or was she with you?"

"What the hell? Of course, she wasn't with me when I was kidnapped! She was in here resting."

"Hmm. Okay. I was just curious about her whereabouts during all of this."

"Look, Jerry, I understand you're doing your best to help me and I really do appreciate everything you have done for me. But suspecting Clara as my kidnapper is crazy."

"Okay, okay," Jerry said calmly. "I'm just trying to cover all my bases. Don't worry about it. You really don't have an idea of who set this up then?"

"No, I don't have a clue. I never thought something like this would happen to me. I can't think of anyone who would try to harm me."

"Hmm, okay," Jerry said thoughtfully, stroking his mustache.

"It just seems…strange, don't you think? Like you said, it was during the middle of the day when anyone could have witnessed it. The kidnapper stole my car and they clearly didn't research the car, since I was able to find the emergency escape latch." Jackson paused, thinking about all the details more. His eyes lit up with a sudden realization. "What if whoever did this wasn't trying to harm me? What if they never planned on killing me? Maybe they were just trying to scare me."

"That's a possibility, especially since a lot of the details don't add up."

"Well, whether or not that was their intention, it worked. Consider me officially terrified."

Jerry smiled gently, patting Jackson on the shoulder. "Hey, you have me and the NYC police on your side, bud. We will get this mess sorted out. I've been a private detective for a long time and I've handled stranger cases than this one."

"Thanks, Jerry. I really appreciate everything you have done for me. I don't know what I would have done if you hadn't stopped to help me that day."

"You're tough, Jackson. I'm sure you would have figured it out."

Jackson tried to adjust his position on the couch to get more comfortable and winced from the pain of moving. "Ah. I swear those painkillers are barely helping."

"I'm sorry to have come over unannounced," Jerry said, standing. "I asked you everything I needed to know for now, but I'll call you if I think of anything else. I'll head out so you can get some rest."

"Thanks, Jerry. I have faith that you will solve the case."

"I'll certainly do my best."

***

Jackson spent the next few days at home recovering against his wishes. Officer Wilson made sure he was safe. No other incidents occurred. On the third day after the traumatic experience, Edgar stopped by to check on Jackson and brought him one of his favorite foods, sushi.

"Ah, man! I've been craving sushi," Jackson said in appreciation, hugging Edgar with one arm for a moment, and immediately popping the container open.

Edgar smiled. "You're welcome."

Clara stood next to Jackson, peering into the container. "Gross!"

Edgar grabbed a piece of sushi from the container and laughed heartily at the appalled look on Jackson's face. "Hey, I bought it."

Jackson finished eating all the sushi within minutes, only allowing Edgar to take one more piece. "Thanks for stopping by.

How has rehearsal been?"

"Oh, you know. It's weird without you there."

"Awww," Clara said in a taunting tone. "Edgar misses having his bestie at work with him!"

Jackson cracked up and turned to nudge Edgar, who had a strangely unfamiliar look on his face. "What?" He asked, stopping mid-laugh.

"Nothing," Edgar responded. "Anyways, I just wanted to make sure you were alright. I better head out now."

"What?" Jackson said again, slightly confused. Edgar lived on the opposite side of town, so it was weird that he had come all the way to Jackson's apartment just for a few minutes, especially with how shitty traffic in NYC was continuously. "You don't want to stay? We were going to grab dinner at that Italian place on the corner. You should come with us."

"Yeah, please!" Clara chimed in. "We want you to."

Edgar thought about it for a moment. "Well, okay. I suppose."

"You're not a third wheel, I promise. We like having you with us!" Clara said in a cheerful voice. "You're Jackson's best friend and after knowing you for so long, I consider you one of my friends too."

Jackson beamed at Clara. She really is great, he thought. She always makes him feel included.

"I'm glad," Edgar replied, surprising Clara by hugging her.

Jackson joined in and soon the three were wrapped in a group hug, each content and happy in their own way.

"Okay, enough sappy shit for one night! I'm starving," Jackson broke away from the hug and headed towards the door.

"Wait, I need a coat," he said, going into his bedroom to search for one.

Edgar smiled at Clara, forcing himself to find something to say. Even though he had known Clara for years now, they still never knew what to talk about during the rare occurrences when Jackson left them alone together. "So, how's life?"

"Great," she responded pleasantly, tucking her long blonde hair behind her ears, causing Edgar to notice the gigantic diamond sparkling on her left ring finger. "I'm excited to plan the wedding! Jackson and I are so happy you're going to be the best man. What about you? How have you been?"

"Great," he responded cheerfully, echoing her response. "Things are really great. Work is good, you know, I love the show." He paused for a moment. "That's a gorgeous engagement ring," he complimented her. "Jackson must have spent a fortune on it," he said, chuckling.

"Thanks, I'm kind of in love with it!" Clara responded, holding out her left hand and admiring the ring. "And I'm glad you enjoy being on the show! That was incredibly nice of Jackson to help you get the role. He's always thoughtful."

"Yeah, that's just like Jackson!" Jackson joined in, entering the room with his wool peacoat now on, causing Edgar and Clara to look at each other and burst out laughing. "Ready to head out?"

The three of them spent the rest of the evening in an unlikely state of euphoria, drunk on their shared relief that Jackson was okay, and that life was great, and they were all great... And there may have been a *small* amount of alcohol involved.

***

Edgar woke up on the leather couch in Jackson (and Clara's) apartment. He sat up, his head throbbing from the excessive alcohol consumption the night before. "Ugh, how much did I drink?" He wondered aloud.

"Too much," Jackson responded with a lighthearted grin. He was sitting at the kitchen table reading the newspaper. Edgar knew he always read the sports section and the comics. He didn't stay up to date on many current events; Edgar had always done that for him.

"Ah. Sorry for crashing here," Edgar responded.

"Don't worry about it. My apartment was much more convenient than making you take a taxi all the way across town. How much do you remember?" Jackson asked.

"I don't know. We were at the restaurant. We shared a few bottles of wine...we were having a great time."

"Yeah. It was a fun night. I appreciate you going out with us. I know Clara can be a lot to handle sometimes, but you were nice to her, so thank you. I think you guys even bonded a little."

"Really? That's great. You know all I want is for you to be happy. And if she makes you happy, then I hope you two have a long married life together," Edgar said sincerely. "Till death do you part."

"Thanks, man. That means a lot. I'm glad you're going to be a part of the wedding too. It wouldn't be the same without you."

"Yeah, of course," Edgar said. "I wouldn't miss it for anything."

"Edgar, I know I probably don't say this enough, but you're the best friend I've ever had. I don't know how I would have gotten through- You've always been there, always had my back... And well, you know I appreciate everything," Jackson finished awkwardly.

Edgar smiled before responding. "Hey, you have always been a good friend too. There's nothing I wouldn't do for you. I hope you know that."

"So, do you need some aspirin or what?"

"That's probably a good idea," Edgar said. "Where's Clara? Still in bed?"

"No, she actually went out with a friend for brunch. Want me to make you some breakfast?"

"You cook?" Edgar said in disbelief. "I seem to remember our years as college roommates differently. What was it you always used to eat? Domino's and Doritos?"

"Yeah, yeah," Jackson replied amicably. "Okay, Chef Edgar, how about you whip up some breakfast for us then?"

"Well, if you insist," Edgar responded, swallowing the aspirin and walking into the kitchen. He scouted out the cupboards and fridge, pausing for a minute. "Uh, how do eggs and toast sound?"

Jackson laughed heartily. "Yeah, okay. But I win."

***

First day back on the set, Jackson thought. *I wonder how they've been doing without me.* He steeled himself and finally entered the building. It felt harder than usual to force his body up the stairs and through the imposing double doors. Part of it was because he was still recovering from his injuries. Both Clara and Edgar had tried to convince him to go to the hospital or at least see a doctor to make sure none of his bones were broken, but he had steadfastly refused until he realized he could still barely walk after several days.

As he entered the spacious room which contained the set of *Dispatching David*, everyone in attendance swiveled to stare at him. Jackson tried not to limp, but everyone already knew what had happened, so it didn't matter. He stepped past the staged apartment room which contained an ugly, worn red couch, a dinged-up coffee table, and several mismatched armchairs of varying colors, shapes, and sizes. Gus ran over to him and surprised him by wrapping an arm around him for a split second. It was one of those so-quick-you-wonder-if-it-even-happened kind of hugs, but still so unlike Gus's perpetual angry, asshole personality.

"We're happy to have you back, princess!" Gus said, stepping away. "It's about time you got your ass back here. We're extremely behind now, so thanks a lot for almost getting yourself killed!" He exclaimed, his face turning redder and redder with each word.

Well, the kindness had lasted a second at least.

"I'm glad to be back, Gus," Jackson said, forcing himself to smile. But the truth was he didn't feel particularly enthusiastic about finishing the show. He was still exhausted and sore, not to mention extremely drugged with painkillers. "Where did we leave off?"

"We've been practicing your scenes with Edgar as your stand-in. But we waited to film until you were back. So, are you all set to go?"

"To start filming? Right now?" Jackson said in a panic. He had thought Gus would let him ease back into things, that maybe next week they could start filming again.

"When did you think I meant, princess?! You're back today, so you're going to work! You've had plenty of time to practice your lines, so I expect nothing short of perfection today. You've been given much more time than the other actors who have been working the past few days!"

"Oh. Okay." Jackson walked onto the set and stood in a random place. He didn't even know which scene they were doing today.

"What the hell do you think you're doing? You don't start the scene in the apartment! You walk in as the lights go up!" Gus exploded.

Shit. Right. Okay, I can do this. I don't have a choice.

Jackson walked off the set and exhaled deeply, preparing for the chaos that was sure to commence as soon as Gus realized he had no idea what was going on. He exhaled again, completely unsure of himself, wondering why he didn't even want to be at work today. On a typical day, Gus yelled at him, berated him, and pointed out every wrong move he made. But normally, it didn't bother him very much. Today everything felt like a personal attack. Jackson knew he had to get through the next few days, then he would be done with the show forever and he wouldn't have to deal with Gus anymore. Maybe he would even take a break from acting. For some reason, it didn't feel like his heart was in it anymore.

The lights went up on the fake apartment and Jackson walked onto the set. He sat on the real couch and said his lines with as much energy as he could muster. Gus yelled several real insults and Jackson's self-esteem and faith in himself steadily fell as the day went on. Finally, finally, it was time for a lunch break.

"Get out of here for an hour, you pathetic excuses for actors!" Gus said, looking like he was going to implode. "My mother could do better than you and she's dead!"

Jackson sat on the couch, with a forlorn look in his eyes. He was holding his copy of the script, mumbling his lines to himself with one last effort to memorize them before the lunch break was over. Edgar joined him on the couch and patted him on the shoulder.

"Hey, how are you doing today?" Edgar asked. He had just come into work. He didn't have a scene until after their lunch break, so luckily, he had missed the morning's embarrassment for Jackson.

"Not so great. I can't remember any of my lines. Taking four days off was an awful idea. Gus is probably going to fire me if I don't get this scene right today." Jackson sighed and ran his hands through his closely cropped dark hair. "I should have been running lines all week. I wasn't thinking..."

Edgar cut him off. "Stop doing this to yourself. Gus is not going to fire you! The show is almost over. Besides, as hard as he is on you, on all of us, he's the one who made the choice for us to be on the show. You went through something extremely traumatic. You had every right to take a few days off to recover. You never take a break. Gus needs to be more understanding." He grabbed the script from Jackson's hands. "Here. I'll run the scene with you a few times, then we're going to Shake Shack for lunch, so you can relax before Gus gets so angry he blows your brains out."

"Thanks, man. I don't know what's wrong with me. I can't get into the scene. Normally, I memorize my lines and after a while I can imagine being the character. By the time we start shooting a scene, I don't have any trouble pulling myself into the world the character lives in. But right now, I feel too much like Jackson Birkman to pretend to be someone else."

"Just remember you aren't Jackson when you're in here. You get to be someone else in this room. Pull yourself back into David's world and don't let yourself escape until you're satisfied. Screw Gus. Everyone knows he's a dick. Now let's run the scene."

Edgar ran lines with him several times and Jackson felt his confidence in his acting abilities slowly seeping back into his being.

"You've got this," Edgar promised. "Prove Gus wrong. You're a talented actor; that's why he asked you to do the show. Remind him why he hired you."

And as the lights went up, Jackson's persona vanished. He *was* David Hoffman, the jerk who slept with Kevin's wife. He was a complicated person who thought he had found love with someone who happened to be his best friend's wife. Sure, he had screwed up, but he felt remorseful now.

"Well, it was better than earlier," Gus remarked as the scene ended. "Not perfect, but it was something."

Jackson smiled for the first time that day. 'Not perfect' was just about the nicest compliment Gus had ever given. "Thanks, Gus. Tomorrow will be better," he promised.

"Damn right it will be! Tomorrow was supposed to be the second to last day of filming the show," he yelled. "We're more behind than I imagined, and this show is looking more and more dreadful by the minute! Everyone better be here by 7 a.m. sharp tomorrow and be prepared to stay late. I don't care what you have going on this weekend. Bring sleeping bags if you have to. We aren't leaving the set until this thing is done!"

"What?" Jackson asked, in an unbelieving tone. "But that was the original schedule. Before..." He couldn't bring himself to say, 'Before I was kidnapped and almost murdered by a psychopath.'

"The TV station doesn't care and neither do I! We promised the fans we would deliver the series finale and we are going to keep that promise if it kills us!" He finished, dramatically, throwing his arms up into the air, and spinning around.

It was evident Gus was serious about finishing the remainder of the show over the weekend. The actors and crew members left the building in a terrified state, each preparing themselves for a grueling weekend, possibly one of the most tiring of their lives. But none were so terrified as Jackson, the star of the show, the one everyone was counting on to shine for the highly anticipated ending.

***

Most of the weekend passed in a blur for everyone involved in *Dispatching David*. Gus turned out to be serious about staying the night in the building, so they all sprawled out around the room, some people with blankets and pillows or air mattresses, others simply using their coats as a balled-up head rest for a few hours of much needed sleep. Well, everyone except Gus. He would never sleep on the floor in a drafty, ancient building. He went home to his lofty, expansive apartment on the Upper East Side and came back each morning refreshed and alert, ready to tackle the day. The rest of the group tread on wearily, forcing themselves through the weekend, hoping their determination and perseverance would pay off. Gus had vastly overestimated how much they would be able to accomplish in one weekend. They still had three scenes of the show left to finish during the next week.

Meanwhile, Officer Wilson knocked on the apartment one morning right as Clara and Jackson were preparing to leave for work.

"Morning, Officer," Jackson answered the door cheerfully.

"Hello, Jackson. Clara. I have news about your car. We traced it for fingerprints and..."

"Well, what is it? Who stole Jackson's car?" Clara interrupted.

Officer Wilson eyed Clara with obvious displeasure. "And we discovered there were several sets of fingerprints in your car. Yours, Clara's, and the fingerprints of your friend you mentioned, Edgar Peterson."

"Oh okay," Jackson said. "So that means whoever stole my car was wearing gloves, so their fingerprints couldn't be traced. Is there another way you can figure out who did it?"

Officer Wilson pursed her lips. "Is there a possibility Edgar could be the one responsible for this? Is there any reason he would want to harm you?"

"What? No! Of course not. Edgar is the nicest... this is ridiculous! It wasn't Edgar."

"You need to answer honestly so we can solve this case. Do you have any enemies? Any secrets from your past? Does anyone know something they could use against you?"

"It's probably just some deranged fan!" Clara said, annoyed. "All that matters is that Jackson is home and he's safe. Plus, with you and the other police officers keeping an eye on our apartment, nothing can happen."

"That's the problem," Officer Wilson replied somberly. "Without any more evidence, or an inkling of a suspect, we don't have much to go on. It makes it difficult for us to continue the case. We need something substantial. The police department is much too short-staffed… Unfortunately, we will have to pull the police officers from the 24-hour surveillance on your apartment. I'm sorry, Jackson, but we are doing the best we can. I hope to be in touch soon." She turned to leave the apartment.

"Can't you stay?" Clara begged. "Please? We feel much safer with you around."

"I'm sorry. The Police Chief has told us we can no longer spend our time here."

"Please. What if they come back? We aren't safe!"

"If anything happens, give me a call. I wish I could continue the surveillance here, but I can't without the permission of the Police Chief. I'm doing my best to help you and I won't stop until I find out who did this to you. Have a good weekend and stay safe," she said, exiting the apartment before they could convince her to stay.

"Jackson, what are we going to do?" Clara sobbed, throwing herself into his arms. "I don't feel safe anymore. I was trying to be strong for you, but I'm scared."

Jackson hugged her tightly and stroked her long blonde hair. "I know, Clara. I know. I'm scared too. But all we can do is try to forget about this awful experience and move on. I don't know how, but we will find a way together."

By the time it was Monday, the start of a fresh week, Jackson finally seemed to grasp David Hoffman's persona again and Edgar had proven himself worthy of his character, Kevin. They had both grown as actors the past several years and they knew it was partly because of their friendship. When you share a profession with your best friend, it can be easy to grow jealous, to begin worrying more about the fame and fortune than the important aspects: striving for greatness and following through with your dreams and ambitions. Edgar and Jackson seemed to accomplish all of this with their careers. However, as excited as Jackson was to almost be done with the show, that's how disappointed Edgar was to nearly be done with it. They had both dreamed of an opportunity like this ever since they had gone to an acting camp together in middle school.

Edgar remembered how awful Jackson used to be at memorizing lines. Since he was such a great friend, he had shown him all his useful tips. He taught Jackson that it wasn't necessarily reciting the exact words in the script that was important, but it was more about staying within the realm of what the writer had intended. The original meaning had to be evident or the sacredness between writer and actor was destroyed. Edgar realized this, among other things, like how practice was key. You had to believe the lines, or the audience wouldn't believe them. Edgar thought he understood the world of acting better than Jackson. When their acting camp had culminated with a play at the end of the summer after sixth grade, Jackson had been the star of the show. As Edgar stood backstage helping with props, he watched his best friend steal the spotlight from their sixth-grade peers. Each audience member's view gravitated towards Jackson, unintentionally neglecting the other actors. There was something irresistible about his presence, even as a 12-year-old actor. Jackson spoke clearly and confidently, not merely reciting lines, but speaking words that were true. As Jackson used every helpful trick Edgar had taught him, Edgar stared from backstage, until he was yelled at by the props master for neglecting his duties. He had stomped angrily back to the props table and destroyed most of the props. Ah, to be young and envious.

But he had changed since then. He had supported Jackson through all his endeavors, acting and otherwise. And he had been rewarded. The day Jackson approached him with the potential role on *Dispatching David* had been one of the greatest days of Edgar's life.

Back then, Edgar was living in the Midwest, far away from the hustle and bustle of NYC where Jackson resided. They had lived halfway across the country from each other for a few years while Jackson's professional acting career took off and Edgar struggled to find work. In those years, Edgar worked as a high school theatre teacher because it was the only job he had been able to get that was involved with theatre. He didn't know what was worse: not being able to act professionally and feeling like a failure or dealing with the constant drama of teaching high-schoolers.

Jackson had visited him one winter when he had a break in between filming seasons of *Dispatching David*. He and Clara were on a break, so Jackson wanted to go out with Edgar to a crappy bar and drink cheap beer. Edgar preferred red wine, but he went along anyways so he could spend time with his best friend. After they left the bar that night, Jackson felt nauseous because he had far surpassed his limit with drinking. Edgar gave up his bed so Jackson could go to sleep and was just placing a blanket over Jackson when Jackson grabbed Edgar's arm to stop him from leaving.

"Dude, I just remembered- Gus is about to start the casting process for a few new characters on *Dispatching David*. I convinced him to let you audition for one of the roles. You would be acting with me for a lot of your scenes. It would be so awesome!"

"What? Are you serious?" Edgar smiled with trepidation, not wanting to get his hopes up yet.

"Yup. You can fly back to NYC with me next week for the audition."

"Holy shit, Jackson! A little warning would have been nice…"

"Sorry, Edgar. I completely forgot about it until just now."

"I know, but I'm going to have to take time off work for the audition. I can't just leave without finding a substitute teacher."

"Edgar…can I say something?"

Edgar sighed, already anticipating what Jackson was going to say. "Sure."

Jackson wearily rubbed his eyes. "You should quit your job anyways. Even if you don't get this role. Quit and move to NYC with me. You can crash in my apartment for awhile if you need to. It will be just like old times!"

"You know what? You're right. I hate my job, I'm miserable, there is nothing left for me here. I'll quit first thing tomorrow."

"Yeah? You mean it?" Jackson was slightly shocked that it had been so easy to convince Edgar. Usually it took him awhile to talk Edgar into making a decision, especially one as impulsive and risky as this one.

"Absolutely. I'll move to NYC, audition for the role, and fucking nail it!" Edgar said, becoming more excited as he thought about the possibility.

"Hell yeah!" Jackson smiled, glad he could help his oldest friend.

Besides, Edgar had to be lonely living here by himself. He didn't have any other friends that Jackson knew of and it didn't seem like he was as close to his family as he used to be. Jackson assumed something had caused a rift between them, but he had never asked because it was none of his business. If Edgar chose to tell him, then that was fine, but if he didn't, it didn't matter.

The next week Edgar flew to NYC with Jackson. He auditioned, got a callback, had a second callback, and finally landed the role. And he never looked back.

CHAPTER 6

This was it. The final episode. *Dispatching David* was a murder mystery TV show that took place in Chicago. The show mainly revolved around David's career and his not-so-stellar life choices. He was a detective who was known for taking on difficult cases. The more gruesome or horrific the case was, the more interested he was in being involved. David was not a nice guy, but he was charismatic and handsome, so people were drawn to him anyways. David was perpetually single, going from one fling to another. His best friend and partner was Kevin, the role played by Edgar. Kevin's role had been played by an actor named Clive for the first few seasons of the show, but Clive's alcoholism had consumed his life, resulting in a DUI and Gus finally firing him from the show. Clive was bitter about being fired and had tried hanging around the set for weeks, until Gus had gotten the police involved and a restraining order was placed, so he could no longer harass Gus and the cast and crew members of the show.

Kevin had been happily married for seven years (or so he thought), until he arrived home one night with dinner he had picked up for himself and his wife, Mary.

"Action!" Gus yelled.

Lights up. Camera rolling. Kevin entered the kitchen, setting the bag containing several Chinese take-out boxes on the white marble counter.

"Mary?" He called out. Usually when he arrived home from work, Mary was in the living room reading and enjoying a glass of wine. That was how she was spending her evenings lately. "Mary, I brought Chinese food for dinner!"

Kevin kicked off his shoes and walked down the hallway into their bedroom. He heard what sounded like grunting and a moan, so he paused uncertainly by the closed bedroom door. Was Mary watching porn? He knocked on the door and heard Mary say, "Shit!"

"What the fuck?" Kevin screamed.

David jumped up from the bed, wrapping the blanket around his torso so his muscular chest was apparent. "Kevin, listen, just calm down. We can talk about it if you give me a chance to explain."

Mary jumped up from the bed, completely naked, frantically searching for her clothes.

"Explain what? How I just got home from a late night of working to find you fucking my wife?" Kevin said, spit flying from his mouth in anger.

"It's not as bad as you think, man. This is all a huge misunderstanding-"

"Nope. Definitely not. I completely understand that you both betrayed me."

"Kevin, I'm so sorry," Mary said, sobbing and covering her mouth with her hand.

"You're not sorry yet, but you will be. I'm going to make you both regret that you ever crossed me." Kevin replied, picking up the wine bottle sitting on the nightstand and throwing it at the wall, so it shattered near Mary's head.

Mary screamed and ran towards David, cowering behind him. David reached out a protective arm to shield her.

"You don't understand, Kevin! This isn't just a meaningless fling. I wasn't screwing her to piss you off. We've been spending a lot of time together lately. Mary has been there for me since my mom died. I felt like I didn't have anyone to turn to. I don't know how I would have gotten through it without her. And...I love her," David said.

"You love her?" Kevin laughed harshly. "David, you don't have a clue what love is. You don't care about anyone except yourself and you just proved that by sleeping with your supposed best friend's wife. You destroyed my marriage and the only real friendship you had. I hope you're happy. Now get the fuck out of my house!" Kevin screamed, advancing towards David.

"Okay, okay," David said quickly, backing away and beginning to put on his clothes. "I'll leave. But whenever you calm down, I want to talk."

"I'm done talking to you. Now leave before I really get mad."

"Fine, I'm leaving. Just...call me when you're ready."

David gathered his belongings and walked towards the

doorway of the bedroom, where Kevin was standing. Kevin lunged towards him and punched him on the nose. David heard a loud snap and groaned, grabbing his nose in pain. His nose was probably broken. He unsuccessfully tried to cover the blood spurting out.

"Okay, man. I deserved that. Do you feel better now?" David said, wiping the blood from his nose with the back of his hand.

"Not yet," Kevin responded, punching David again, this time in the stomach.

David groaned again, doubling over from the impact.

Mary cried out. "Stop, Kevin! Stop it!"

Kevin laughed viciously. "Oh, sure, now you have something to say, Mary. You don't want me to hurt your lover?"

Mary sobbed. "Kevin, please…"

"Please what, Mary?"

"Please don't hurt him," she responded in a muffled tone, sobbing uncontrollably.

"Don't you think he deserves to be taught a lesson, Mary? People can't just go around sleeping with other people's wives and not suffer any consequences. The world doesn't work that way. The world isn't a fair place. So, if I decide he needs to be punished for his betrayal, then I have the right to deal out that punishment. Understand?"

Mary nodded, still quietly sobbing, not wanting to upset her husband even more. She had never seen him like this and was terrified of what he was going to do next.

David was trying to make himself stand so he could leave. He realized it wasn't the right time to try to reason with Kevin. He didn't blame him for being angry; he just didn't consider what would happen when Kevin found out. David wasn't used to being forced to take responsibility for his actions when he screwed up. Usually, he could get away with it. But he also knew that this was probably the shittiest thing he had ever done.

Kevin smacked David on the back of his head, causing him to fall to the floor yet again. David groaned, holding his head and trying to get his bearings. He needed to get out of Kevin's house now. He realized with how upset Kevin was, he might just keep attacking until he killed him.

"Okay, okay. Kevin, please- I'm sorry. I'll leave."

David forced himself to stand despite his injuries and dragged himself once again towards the bedroom door. This time Kevin let him pass, his eyes glinting with anger.

"I'm letting you go, but this is far from over."

"I understand. Thank you."

David limped to the front door and Kevin slammed the door shut after he left, sprinting back towards the bedroom. Mary was cleaning up the spilled wine and broken glass from the wine bottle.

"Worry about the mess later," Kevin told her.

"Okay." Mary stood from her bent position and set down the rag she was using to soak up the wine from the hardwood floors. "Kevin, I'm sorr-" she started to say.

"Stop. I know you're not or you wouldn't have done it. You clearly thought about it. He's my best friend, Mary! I think it almost would have been better if it was a random guy, but David? Why did it have to be him?" Kevin sat on the bed, looking crestfallen, his anger dissipating.

"It just…it just happened. I promise I didn't plan on sleeping with him. Like David was saying, we started spending more time together because he needed someone to talk to after his mom died. I was only trying to console him at first. It went too far. You were working all those late nights. I was so lonely without you here..."

"That's a load of bullshit," Kevin said. "David and I are partners. We work similar hours. Besides, you knew about my career before we got married. You knew what you were getting into. I thought you understood what our life would be like together. I thought you were okay with it because you knew I was solving cases, helping people, trying to establish that the greater good will triumph over evil. I thought we were on the same page."

"That isn't fair. Of course I knew you were a detective and that it would be difficult not seeing you as much as I would like to, but I underestimated how much I would worry about you. Every single day when you leave for work, I think about how dangerous your job is and I wonder if you're going to come home. I wonder if your good morning kiss will be the last one I will ever have from you. When you're working late and I haven't heard from you, I toss and turn waiting for a phone call or a knock on the door from someone telling me that you've been killed. You can't imagine what it's been like all these years, always wondering if you're dead."

"I'm constantly checking in on you. Every day, I ask you to tell me about your day. I'm always making sure you're doing okay and that I'm there for you enough." At that moment, something struck Kevin and he felt as if his heart had irrevocably shattered. "You've been lying to me. You haven't really been happy, have you?

Mary hesitated, staring at the floor, unable to meet Kevin's eyes. "I'm not always unhappy," she said slowly, carefully choosing her words. "I don't want to hurt you. I never meant for things to end this way."

Kevin felt tears welling in his eyes. He couldn't remember the last time he was reduced to tears. Probably during his first case. A young, single mother who murdered her three children. He had been one of the first people to reach the scene. He could still remember how sick and angry he felt upon the sight of those three small children, laying in the backyard next to the pool, faces blue and clothes soaking wet. The mother had thrown them in the pool, one by one, and laughed manically as she explained what she had done. David had been at the scene with him, but it wasn't David's first case and he seemed remarkably unaffected by the horrific sight. David had a talent for overlooking such gruesome sights and focusing on the details and facts of the case instead, getting done whatever he needed to do.

"Kevin?" Mary said softly, placing her hand on his arm.

Kevin jerked away, not wanting Mary to touch him since she was touching his best friend not too long ago.

"Kevin," she said again.

"Yes, Mary?" He said coldly. He felt as if all his usual warmth towards his wife had evaporated. She had fooled him. And for how long? Did he want to know?

"We can talk more tomorrow after we both get some rest. Things always seem better in the morning when the light of a new day has dawned."

"Fine. You can take the bed. I'll sleep in the guest room," Kevin replied.

Mary's lip quivered. "You don't want to sleep with me tonight?"

"You didn't leave me a choice."

***

The gun was aimed directly at David's head.

"Don't do it," he pleaded, tears streaming down his face. "Please. I can fix this. You-you're my best friend. If there's anything I can do to make it up to you..."

Edgar pulled the trigger on the GLOCK 22. And with that, the gun went off, the noise echoing throughout the building. A bullet travelled through the air unexpectedly as Jackson stared in horror, not moving quickly enough to avoid the impact. The bullet sliced through the front of Jackson's head and escaped on the other side before he could react. Chunks of his head shattered at the bullet's contact and flew to the ground with a splat, his body crumpling and falling soon after. Edgar stared openmouthed at Jackson's body, flinging the gun away so that it clattered onto the stage.

Someone screamed. All the actors and crew members rushed onto the set, flocking toward the scene. One crew member even ran out of the bathroom still zipping up his pants.

"Oh my God," Edgar exclaimed. "Oh my God, what happened?! Someone do something! Why isn't anyone doing anything?!" He rushed over to Jackson's body and fell to the ground, checking Jackson's pulse in a futile attempt to make sense of the situation. He pulled Jackson's body toward him, the blood from the open wound in the front of Jackson's head cascading freely. Edgar screamed and began to sob hysterically. "He's dead, he's dead, he's dead," he moaned continuously, rocking back and forth on his heels.

Gus stood from his director's chair at the front of the room and briskly walked over to Jackson and Edgar. He gently grabbed Jackson's arm, blood spurting across his Ralph Lauren shirt. He checked for a pulse on Jackson's wrist and whipped out his cell phone, immediately dialing 911. "There's been an accident," he said in the quietest voice he had ever spoken. "773 Creston Avenue." A pause. "No. There's no need for that. Jackson Birkman is dead."

***

There was an outpour of sympathy and cries of outrage from the fans. There were two differing opinions about Jackson's death; some thought it was suicide, while others assumed it was murder. For those who sided with the idea of suicide, they understood why Jackson would kill himself. Fans of the show knew that Jackson had recently become engaged to his longtime girlfriend. Many people assumed putting off the engagement was Jackson's decision and that he had his reasons for being deeply unhappy, not just in his relationship with Clara but his overall state of life. Suicide made sense. Celebrities discontent with fame and fortune committed suicide all the time after they realized none of it meant anything and that what they thought was the pursuit of happiness was in fact a futile attempt to fill their empty lives. But was that true? Had Jackson been unhappy? Did he have a mental illness? Did he have a dark secret he didn't want everyone to find out?

On the other hand, those who assumed Jackson's death was murder had a multitude of questions as well. Who had switched the guns? How was a real gun not detected on the set? Didn't

Dispatching David take any security precautions? And most importantly, had it been one of them, another actor or crew member, who had thought of the crazy, awful idea? Who would want Jackson Birkman dead and who was gutsy enough to follow through? These questions haunted everyone, but none so much as Clara, who was the most devastated of them all.

"Clara! Clara! Let me in!" Edgar yelled, pounding on the door of Jackson and Clara's apartment.

"Hold on!" Clara answered, rushing to the door and tying her bathrobe. "Oh, Edgar! What are you doing here? Is rehearsal over already?"

"I have something to tell you..." Edgar said, trailing off, unsure of how to continue. How could he even begin to explain to his best friend's fiancée that her soon-to-be betrothed was dead?

"What's going on? Where's Jackson?" Clara asked frantically, looking into the hallway for Jackson.

"Can I come in for a few minutes?"

"Sure," Clara responded, confused. "Is Jackson with you?"

Edgar sighed, still not answering her questions, and followed her to the couch... the couch he had helped Jackson pick out years ago, when he first moved out of his parent's house. They sat in silence, while Edgar contemplated what to say.

"At rehearsal tonight," he began, "there was an accident."

"What kind of accident?" Clara asked, twirling her long blonde hair nervously. "Is Jackson okay?"

"Jackson was shot in the head and died instantly," Edgar blurted out, no longer able to contain the words.

"What? You're kidding, right? This is a joke? Well, it's not funny," Clara said quietly but fiercely, standing up from the couch and swaying uneasily on her feet.

"Clara, sit down. It's okay."

"How can you say that? It's not okay! Jackson is..." She stopped in the middle of forming the words, choking on them. She couldn't bear to finish the sentence. "I don't believe you, Edgar."

"Someone must have switched the gun for the last scene. No one knows who did it or exactly what happened yet. I rushed over here to tell you after I talked to the police. I knew you would rather hear it from me than a stranger." He placed a comforting hand on her shoulder.

At his touch, she fell into his arms, sobbing uncontrollably on his chest. "Jackson can't be dead," she wailed. "We were supposed to get married next year. He was finally going to be my husband. We had our future planned together..."

"I know, Clara. And I'm so incredibly sorry that was taken away from you. I lost...my best friend. The best friend I've ever had. I don't know what I'm going to do without him." He paused, struggling to maintain his composure. He felt tears welling up in his eyes and he knew he was probably going to lose control soon, but he was trying to stay strong for Clara. "But we will both get through this. We are going to find out who did it and make sure they rot in prison for the rest of their life."

Clara sobbed quietly for a few minutes before she was able to respond. "Okay. But once I find out who killed Jackson, I don't think I can bear to know they're still alive. Is that awful? I just don't know who would do this! Everyone loved Jackson! He had thousands of fans, people who sent him love letters and phone numbers and gifts of all kinds. People who begged for signed pictures and t-shirts. They all wanted his attention and admiration, but I had it. I was the woman who won him over and I lost him," Clara rambled, wiping her eyes with the back of her hand and shakily trying to sit up.

"I don't know who would want to harm him. I don't have any answers. I want to figure this out as much as you do."

"God, this is so awful. I never thought I would have to go through something like this. I thought- We would get married and start a family and I would have everything I ever wanted. Now I don't get... any of that." Clara stared off, feeling empty. She didn't know how she would ever recover, much less move on.

"He really loved you," Edgar said simply. "Before you, I honestly never thought he would settle down."

"I had my doubts sometimes too," she said honestly. "But eventually he realized what he wanted. I'm glad he lived long enough to propose to me. At least I know for sure that he did want to be with me. We just didn't get the chance..."

"Clara, I know it's going to be difficult to get through this, but really I'm glad you're here. No one else will understand what we're going through."

"I-I don't want to be alone tonight. Do you want to stay over? You can sleep on the couch," Clara said hesitantly. She had gotten used to Jackson's constant presence and she didn't want to spend her first night without him by herself. Otherwise she would probably end up crying all night and mourning alone wasn't healthy at this stage.

"Sure. I think that's a great idea. You know, I helped him pick out this couch before you two were dating."

"You did?" Clara said, laughing although her cheeks were soaked with tears. "No wonder he won't get rid of it."

"What? You tried to make him get rid of it?!"

"This thing is hideous!" Clara said, hitting the arm of the leather couch. "And ancient."

"Oh, come on. It's not even that old. It's a classic piece of furniture, the kind that never goes out of style!"

"Ha ha. This thing was out of style before my Grandma was born. But, if you're staying the night, we might as well watch a movie to take our minds off it. What do you want to..." Clara started to ask before they said in unison, *Star Wars*.

It had been Jackson's favorite movie series since he first watched it in fifth grade and it seemed the right way to end the incredibly awful night. Tomorrow they would start to go through Jackson's belongings, begin planning the funeral, call Jackson's parents, and go down to the police station to see if any new information had been discovered about Jackson's death. Tonight, all they could do was try to console each other the best they could. They were Jackson's two favorite people; no matter what their relationship had been before, at least for tonight they were all each other had for comfort.

Edgar fell asleep on the couch halfway through the first *Star Wars* movie. Clara was still wide awake. She got up to find a blanket to drape over him, then she climbed into her and Jackson's bed, of which she was now the sole occupant. She laid in the king-sized bed with the 600 thread count sheets and $800 comforter and wondered, what if it was something to do with the money? Jackson complained about his savings dwindling away and not being able to afford a proper engagement ring or wedding, but how could he explain his extravagant lifestyle which had never suffered throughout his so-called debt? What if he owed someone a lot of money and hadn't been able to pay it back? Clara wondered, finally beginning to drift to sleep. But it wasn't a peaceful sleep. It was the first night of many restless nights yet to come.

CHAPTER 7

I carefully opened the front door to the majestic, towering, old building *Dispatching David* was filmed inside. Stealing a spare key from the janitor and making a copy had been far too easy. It was just after midnight and I knew there weren't any security cameras. The alarm had already been deactivated. I had triple checked every detail. Nothing stood in my way now. I tiptoed inside, practically holding my breath as I walked down the hallway to the set of the show. My footsteps echoed in the darkness. I fumbled for the light switch with my gloved hand, so I could make my way to the backstage area. I knew all the props were stored backstage. As the light slowly flickered on and my eyes adjusted to the light, I held the brown paper bag tightly and continued walking.

I flipped on another light switch to illuminate the backstage area and spotted the fake GLOCK 22 sitting on the shelf. The taped label in front of it read, "Kevin's gun." I opened the brown paper bag, which crinkled loudly as I pulled out a real GLOCK 22. It was already loaded and ready to go. I held it in my hand for a moment. It wasn't a particularly heavy gun, but it felt heavy in my hands just then. Maybe it was the weight of what I knew was coming. I made sure the safety was on and set it on the shelf, grabbing the fake gun to take with me.

I walked onto the stage and stood in the center, holding the fake gun, breathing heavily. I stared into the dark abyss on the other side of the building and held up the gun, aiming into the blackness.

CHAPTER 8:
Edgar

Edgar stood on the set of *Dispatching David*, staring into the camera, although it was off and no one was recording. He swayed on his feet, his legs suddenly unsteady. The room felt like it was spinning around him.

"The show must go on!" Gus exclaimed manically. "Edgar, you will take over as David. We only have a few scenes left. We aren't cheating the dedicated fans from the ending they have been waiting to see for five years!"

Edgar stared back at Gus stoically for a minute. "That's the first time you've ever referred to me as something other than princess."

"This is a serious issue. Think about it and be honest with me. Do you want the role?" Gus asked.

"Of course not. I could never do that. It wouldn't be right. I'm still in mourning. It just happened yesterday for God's sake! I can't believe you're even forcing us to be on set today. This is insane. Do you expect me to just go on camera and pretend to be David, knowing it was supposed to be Jackson out there finishing what he started? He never even had a chance..." Edgar cried.

"We're so damn close, Edgar! Just two scenes left. Jackson's death is tragic, but we are getting more publicity than ever. The series finale is expected to have millions of viewers watching live as David finally gets what he deserves. Isn't that what you've always wanted, to be the lead? I've seen you coveting Jackson's role. Well, now is your chance! Seize the opportunity!" Gus said, becoming more and more agitated as he spoke.

"Is the publicity all you care about? Jackson is dead!" Edgar screamed. "He's dead and I'm the one who shot the gun that killed him! Do you know how that makes me feel? I don't know who switched the guns, but if I ever find out, I swear to God, I will kill them."

"Calm down, Edgar. At least consider it."

"I don't know, Gus. Who would take over my role?" Edgar asked hesitantly. "I know it's only two scenes, but it should have been Jackson finishing as the lead. I wish he could have finished the show."

"The whole situation is tragic. I'm heartbroken over it. And you- you were his best friend. It wouldn't be right if anyone else took over the role. No one will find it strange if you're the replacement. You were his biggest fan and viewers will think it's sweet that you're willing to finish the show, while going through such a rough time. Besides, if you do this, I'll get you any acting gig you want. Anything you can dream of, it's yours," Gus promised, with a huge grin on his face.

"Alright," Edgar agreed at last. "But I'm not doing it for the fans, or the money, or the prestige. I'll help you finish the show, but it's for Jackson. I know he enjoyed being David; all he ever wanted was to be an actor, even when we were kids. That's all he ever talked about. This is my tribute to him."

"Then it's settled. We can finish filming this week and air the last episode as soon as possible. Everyone is going to be overjoyed!"

"What will Clara think?" Edgar wondered aloud. "Will she be angry with me?"

"No, no, of course not! Clara will be happy that you're the one finishing what Jackson started. She will understand that it should be you."

"Of course. You're- you're absolutely right. It should be me."

"The perfect ending! The show will have the ending it deserves and I will be known as the greatest director of all time!" Gus said manically, smiling at Edgar. Probably for the first time. "And you will be the actor who is remembered as the greatest of his time. You can have any role you want after this. Just imagine it. Your name in lights on Broadway. Thousands of people calling, 'Encore! Encore!' Then lining up after a performance just to catch a glimpse of you or if they're lucky enough, to shake your hand. Your very own star on the Hollywood Walk of Fame."

Edgar said softly, "I suppose I'm the star now."

"What was that, princess? You're mumbling again."

"Nothing, Gus."

Edgar stared into the camera again, imagining himself on

Broadway just like Gus had promised him, the spotlight focused on him, the crowd rising as one to give him a standing ovation.

CHAPTER 8:
Gus

W hat are you-" Gus started to say, but Edgar held up his hand and abruptly interrupted him.

"Please. I know it may seem a little crazy, but I knew Jackson better than anyone. It's what he would have wanted for the show. He's the one who persuaded you to let me audition for this show. He always did whatever he could for me. He had more drive and charm, so he became the famous one. But I know he would have wanted the same for me. He would have given it to me if he could have," Edgar said, insistently.

"I don't know, princess. It doesn't seem right to keep the show going after this. We've gotten a lot of bad publicity. People think the whole thing was planned. That someone wanted to kill him. But who would do that? Who would want Jackson dead?" Gus paced the room, rubbing his moustache anxiously.

"I don't know. I don't understand how anyone could do such

a thing," Edgar said, as tears rolled down his cheeks. He brushed them away and fought to continue speaking, "I'm still shocked and I'm mourning. I can't believe he's gone. But, trust me, I know Jackson would have been happy with me as his replacement. He wouldn't have wanted anyone else to do it. And now I just want this awful thing over as soon as possible. Gus, the last episode was expected to have millions of viewers. Think of how many people will want to watch it now. Even people who weren't fans of the show before will want to see the finale. And we can't play the real ending. So, we have to re-shoot it and I'll be David."

"Maybe you're right. Really, it's just a few scenes, then it's over. We can finish the show and be done with this whole mess," Gus said uncertainly, contemplating the right decision.

"If you don't want to re-shoot the scene, then I would understand completely. Maybe the writers can create a new ending, one that is more suitable."

"No, no. That would never work. The true fans will want to see David die, after all the shit he's done. No one wants him to live."

Edgar waited for Gus to make up his mind, but he already knew he had him convinced.

After an awkward pause, Gus finally responded, "Fine. You can take Jackson's place, but you have to get rid of those fucking awful glasses."

Edgar said softly, "I suppose I'm the star now."

"What was that, princess? You're mumbling again."

"Nothing, Gus."

Edgar had always stayed hidden in the shadows, but he knew

he really was the better actor. Edgar stared into the camera again, imagining himself on Broadway just like Gus had promised him, the spotlight focused on him, the crowd rising as one to give him a standing ovation.

CHAPTER 9:
Clara

Clara woke up the next morning as if in a fog. She dimly remembered the previous night's events but chose to ignore thinking about it for the time being. She had to make herself plan Jackson's funeral and accomplish a dozen other important things because of his death. The worst of which would be calling Jackson's parents. Although, maybe she could beg Edgar to do that. He had known them longer after all.

After she tearfully called Edgar, he agreed to call Jackson's parents. After a brief conversation with them, they booked a flight from Minneapolis to NYC. They had an upscale apartment in downtown Minneapolis, since their two children were adults and had moved out long ago. Their remaining child, Jessica, was 24 and had chosen to stay closer to home. She lived in an apartment 20 minutes away from her parents, but she had never been as close to them as Jackson. Jackson was the oldest and he had been spoiled his entire life. They had paid for dozens of acting camps and classes throughout his youth, a variety of expensive headshots, and even covered the entire cost of his college tuition, where he studied the art of acting in greater detail. His parents wanted only the best for their firstborn and Jessica felt she had gotten shoved aside and neglected. She refused to accompany her parents to NYC right away. Instead, she argued for hours until they eventually convinced her that she needed to be at her brother's funeral, no matter how much she claimed to have hated him. At last, she promised them that she would show up the day before the funeral and return home immediately after it was over. She understood the necessity of being there but didn't want to deal with her parents for any longer than she had to.

Jackson's parents dropped by the apartment unexpectedly when Clara was going through Jackson's belongings. She invited them warmly into her apartment and offered them drinks (water, coffee, or lemonade) and they awkwardly gathered in the sitting room.

"I'm so sorry for your loss," Clara said awkwardly.

"Don't be ridiculous, Clara. You lost him too," Jackson's father, Rick replied.

"Yes, well..." she responded uncertainly, wishing she was anywhere but here. Or that Jackson's sister was with them to diffuse the tension. They had always gotten along well, despite Jackson and Jessica's strained relationship. "Where is Jessica?" She wondered aloud. "Is she flying in later?"

Jackson's mother, Susan, scoffed and flipped her freshly dyed auburn hair over her shoulder. "No. She's being childish, as usual.

She refuses to come to New York until the day of the funeral and she's flying home practically the second it ends. Even after Jackson's death, she still has to make everything about her."

Clara looked at Rick and Susan, unsure of how to proceed with the conversation. This was dangerous territory. Jackson was an expert at dodging their questions. Why couldn't he be here to help her? She felt like screaming as she remembered Jackson was dead and that was why his parents were at her apartment in the first place. "I'm sure it's just hard on her," she finally said. "It's hard for all of us to accept that he's gone. Going to the funeral will only make it more real."

"More *real*?" Susan repeated with disdain as her husband chuckled in a light, airy, but very mocking fashion he had perfected. "Oh, my dear, the situation is all too 'real' to Rick and I. We have lost our only child—our only son and we are heartbroken. This seems like a terrible, terrible nightmare. I keep waiting to wake up, but then I don't, and things only get worse," she said bitterly, choking on a sob.

"I feel the same way," Clara answered softly. "I never thought I would have to endure this. At least not until we had many years of marriage and happiness together, when he had lived his life and was ready to go." She sighed and gazed thoughtfully at the chevron rug in front of her. "We had so many plans for our future."

"Mhm," was the only response from Susan. Susan and Rick raised their glasses of lemonade almost in unison and sipped carefully, their faces making nearly identical expressions of thinly veiled disgust.

"The lemonade is...interesting," Rick said, setting it down on the coffee table.

"It's just instant," Clara said, laughing slightly.

Susan pursed her lips, the epitome of disdain and displeasure. "Well, we came by to go through Jackson's things. We brought a few boxes to bring everything back with us. Is it all in the bedroom?" She asked, standing and peering around nosily.

Jackson's parents had opted for staying at a nearby hotel, instead of staying at Jackson and Clara's apartment, which was perfectly fine with Clara. They had never cared much for Clara, even though Jackson had been with her for over six years. Despite Jackson's protests, his parents were insistent that Clara was only after his money. Although, his parents had essentially cut him off after he graduated from college and he still hadn't learned how to act responsibly with his money. Since he had barely been scraping by financially when he and Clara met, his parents had no reason to worry about Clara stealing anything.

Susan strode into Jackson and Clara's bedroom, staring around helplessly. There were piles of clothes, paperwork, pictures, and childhood memory box items scattered all over the room. "Dear God," his mom exclaimed upon realizing the extent of the mess. "Why is his room in such a state?"

"I started going through his things. You know Jackson, nothing was organized," Clara explained. "I was going to wait until you two were here to get rid of anything, but there's also a lot of junk mixed in with the keepsakes."

Rick entered the bedroom also, staring aghast at the contents of the room. "Did you just say you were going to get rid of it?" He asked in angered astonishment.

"Only the things that weren't important. We can't keep everything," Clara reasoned.

"Maybe some of these 'things' hold no meaning to you, but we want to keep anything that will remind us of our Jackson," Susan said.

"Sorry," Clara responded, scooping up a pile of old receipts, bills, and movie tickets. "If you want all these pointless papers, then be my guest. I'm only keeping the things that matter."

"Excuse me?" Rick replied. "Don't you dare talk to my wife like that. And what exactly makes you think you have a claim on any of Jackson's belongings? You two weren't married yet, so technically we get to keep it all," he said with a nasty smile.

Clara looked around the room, her gaze landing on several framed pictures of her and Jackson, the teddy bear he had given her on their first date, his worn t-shirts he had let her sleep in, and a dozen other things that his parents wouldn't understand the sentimentality she felt towards. "Legally, I may not have the right to keep anything, but I think I deserve to at least take a few small things. Do you really want these framed pictures of us? Or this ratty old hoodie? What are you going to do with it, let it sit in your storage room and gather dust? It's not like it's going to be out on display in your family room." She picked up the items mentioned and put them aside. "Look, if you want it, fine. But we were supposed to get married, so I don't think that means you can just take all of his cars and the rest of his expensive belongings."

"You can't be serious, darling. Of course you don't get to keep his cars. Or the 50-inch flat screen TV, or even his Blu-ray player." Susan began gathering random items into her arms and throwing them into boxes. "Rick, are you going to help me or are you just going to stand there?"

"Yes, dear," Rick said, beginning to grab Jackson's belongings.

Clara felt completely helpless as she watched them take away every last bit of Jackson. Maybe it had been wrong to assume, but of course she wanted to keep it all! If they had gotten married, she would have been the one to get everything. And no, they weren't married, but they had planned on it, and wasn't that close enough anyways? It's not as if she only wanted the expensive things Jackson had owned. She didn't care about the money, no matter what Jackson's parents thought. She just liked the idea of finally owning a few nice things and driving a new car. She worked hard; she deserved to have a reward. Besides, how was she supposed to preserve the memory of Jackson if she didn't have anything of his left to hold onto?

"I know you think I only care about Jackson's money," Clara said calmly. "But I wouldn't have stayed with him for this long if that was all I cared about. And I hope you finally realize how much I loved him, how much I still love him, and that this is just as painful for me as it is for you two. I know you lost your son and I'm sorry. But I lost my soulmate and I don't know how I'm going to ever get over it," she said, tears spilling down her cheeks and staining her crisp maroon blouse. She covered her mouth with her hand to stifle her sobs, but it was too late. Once she started crying, she didn't know how she was ever going to find the will to stop.

Susan wordlessly walked over to Clara. She could count the number of times on one hand that Susan had ever hugged her, but it didn't matter. In that moment, they were going to pretend to get along because they had both lost someone they cared about dearly.

Jackson's parents were slightly more considerate after witnessing Clara's breakdown, but they still insisted on keeping most of Jackson's possessions. It was probably because they didn't want to seem like they were trying to forget him or dishonor his memory. They were all about reputation and cared greatly about what other people thought about them. For Rick and Susan, it was bad enough people knew their son had been shot in the head and killed while filming a TV show, but it would be even worse if people had any reason to dislike them or somehow blame them for the incident.

However, what no one yet realized was the extent of Jackson's troubles. He had kept it hidden from nearly everyone: his family, Clara, and almost everyone else in his life.

***

"You've already asked me the same questions a dozen times. I've told you everything I know! I don't have any new information!" Clara said, tossing one of the sequined throw pillows from the couch on the ground, frustrated.

Officer Wilson watched the pillow sail across the room, but simply smiled kindly in response. "I know this is hard, Clara, but please understand I am only trying to help."

"It's your fault this happened! If you and the other stupid cops hadn't stopped the 24-hour surveillance, maybe Jackson would still be alive, and I wouldn't be planning his funeral!"

"I already told you. It wasn't my idea to stop the surveillance and even if we hadn't, someone still could have found a way to kill him. We are doing the best we can to solve the case and your cooperation is needed throughout this process," Officer Wilson explained.

"I don't care what you need from me! I'm mourning the death of my fiancé and I don't want to talk about this anymore!" Clara screamed, this time picking up a glass vase from the sitting area and preparing to throw it across the room.

Officer Wilson moved quickly, grabbing Clara's wrist to prevent her from throwing the vase. "You don't want to do that," she said, placing the vase back on the end table. "Throwing things won't make this easier; I can promise you that."

Clara sighed deeply and ran her hands through her long blonde hair, as she always did when she was anxious or nervous. "Okay, you're right. What else do you need to know?"

Officer Wilson smiled patiently. "Thank you. I appreciate your help. Do you have any idea how Jackson was paying the rent for his apartment, utilities, and all of the other necessities?"

"Uh, yeah, in case you've forgotten he was kind of famous from the show. He made a pretty decent living," Clara said, sarcastically.

"A pretty decent living. More than that, I would say. But it's interesting...he hasn't had much activity in his bank account lately as far as deposits go." Officer Wilson pulled out several papers from a file in her briefcase. "These documents show how much money has been deposited in his account and how much has been withdrawn for the past several months. Do you understand my confusion?"

"But...there has to be some sort of mistake," Clara said

emphatically. "I don't know exactly how much money he makes, but I know it's at least a hundred thousand dollars per episode. Maybe the bank incorrectly documented the transactions. Or maybe he has multiple bank accounts? I don't know! I only know he has been paying for everything somehow," she insisted.

"Have you ever lent money to Jackson, Clara?"

"No. He has much more money than I do. I'm an editor for a women's magazine. I make enough money to afford living in NYC, but not nearly as much as Jackson."

"Where is all of his money?"

"I have no idea, Officer Wilson. I don't know what's going on, but I don't see how this has anything to do with me."

"We are simply ruling out all of the suspects."

"I'm a suspect? I'm his fiancée! Why would I want to kill Jackson? Tell me, what was my motivation for doing it?"

"Calm down, Clara. It's understandable that you're upset. We have no reason to think you planted the gun. We are simply taking every precaution necessary."

"I didn't do it, I swear! Why would I?" She repeated.

"For the money, the cars. Maybe you weren't getting along well lately. Maybe you had a fight and things escalated and you decided you didn't want to marry him, but you didn't want to back out."

Clara was wide-eyed and astounded. "I would never harm him. I love him. Besides, I don't get anything because we weren't married yet."

"Hm?" Officer Wilson asked, half-listening, while she flipped through the papers laid out on the coffee table.

"Jackson's parents were over here yesterday and they told me I don't get any of Jackson's possessions because we weren't married. We were only engaged, so it's as if our relationship was nothing. It wasn't legally binding, so it's nothing! He's dead, but we weren't married, so I shouldn't care!" Clara screamed, then instantly seemed to calm down again. "I need some alcohol."

She walked over to the fridge and pulled out a bottle of wine. "Want some, Officer Wilson?"

"No, thank you, I'm fine. I don't think you should be drinking while we have this conversation. Perhaps, I'll come back later..." Officer Wilson said cordially, rising to leave.

Clara popped the cork off the wine bottle and began chugging straight from the bottle. She stopped and wiped her mouth with the back of her hand. "Why would you go now? Time for the fun to start!"

"Do you have someone who can come stay with you tonight? It doesn't seem right for you to be alone."

"Edgar," Clara said. "He's Jackson's best friend." She chugged more of the wine. "He always loved Edgar more than me."

"Okay. I think you should call Edgar or one of your other friends and see if someone can join you for the night. I'm sure a friend would be much better company than me." Officer Wilson gathered up her papers and placed them back in her briefcase.

Clara was downing more of the wine and eyeing Officer Wilson's tattered old briefcase as she snapped it shut. "Who carries briefcases anymore anyways? That's such an ancient idea!" Clara exclaimed.

"Call a friend, Clara. I'll be back tomorrow afternoon around

3. Have a good night." Officer Wilson said, opening the front door and leaving the apartment.

Clara's response was to slam the door and knock back the bottle of wine once again. At this rate, she was going to have to buy another bottle.

The Long Shadow on the Stage

CHAPTER 10:
Edgar

Edgar stared into the mirror near the entrance of the apartment. He saw his reflection, but he looked like an ethereal, ghostly version of his former self. His long black hair hung in strands around his face. His eyes had dark circles underneath them from staying awake for several days in a row. He couldn't remember the last time he had eaten or taken a shower. Edgar sighed as he prepared himself. He didn't feel prepared to deal with Clara tonight. He wasn't even equipped to deal with his own shit.

Clara had called Edgar over to comfort her. Officer Wilson had left when Clara started drinking and Clara didn't want to be alone. When he arrived, she was already well into her first bottle of wine and the effects were showing.

"Clara, do you think maybe you should slow down a little?" Edgar asked hesitantly, not wanting to set her off, since she was clearly in a fragile state.

"No, I'm fine. I've barely had any!"

"You've drank almost an entire bottle..." He pointed out.

Clara looked at the bottle, as if noticing how much was gone. "Oh. You're right. Well, we need to get more then."

"I don't think you should be leaving the house like this. You're drunk."

"I'm *not* drunk. I'm fine."

Edgar sighed. "I had to fight through the reporters to get into the apartment building when I got here. Has it been like that since...?" He trailed off.

Clara laughed sarcastically. "Yup. They are out there every day, which is why I have barely left my apartment."

"Yeah, they have been outside my place too. Have you talked to them?"

"Of course not! Have you?"

"No, and I won't. If you really want the wine though, I'll run to the store on the corner and grab another bottle, okay?"

"Better make that two." Clara laughed as she finished the rest of the bottle.

"Okay, fine. I'll be back soon."

Clara stood to throw the wine bottle away and swayed clumsily as she tried to cross the room. "See? I'm fine. I can come with you. Just need to grab my coat and I'm all set."

"Clara, please. Stay in your apartment. I'll only be gone for a few minutes. I don't want something to happen to you. You're safer in here."

"Oh, fine. You're no fun."

Edgar rolled his eyes and exited the apartment. Clara slumped onto the ground in the kitchen, cradling her head in her hands. She felt completely numb. That was why she wanted to drink; couldn't everyone understand that? She didn't want to be in so much pain. After what felt like forever in Clara's drunken state, Edgar came back to the apartment with two bottles of wine, one red and one white.

"I didn't know what your preference was," he explained.

"Normally I like white better. But right now, I'll drink whatever," she answered, hopping up from her spot on the floor and using the corkscrew to pull the corks out of both of the wine bottles.

"Hey, don't open both of them right now," Edgar complained. "What if we don't drink that much tonight?"

"Oh, we will," Clara responded. "Besides, you get a bottle and I get one. It works out perfectly!"

Clara scrolled through her phone's music library and began to play her "Good Mood Music" playlist, which she used in dire times when she needed to be cheered up. Although these weren't the usual circumstances she would turn to this playlist, Clara didn't know where else to turn. "Come on, Edgar! Dance!"

Edgar sighed in reluctance and smiled. "I'm going to need some more wine before I'll dance."

"Then drink up, Edgar! I am determined for us to have fun tonight. We deserve it."

"Okay, okay." Edgar began to drink from the bottle of red wine and Clara jumped up and down in anticipation.

"Shut Up and Dance" by Walk the Moon played from Clara's Galaxy S6 Edge and she became so excited she almost spilled the bottle of wine she was clutching in her right hand. "Oops," she giggled.

"Careful," Edgar warned. "You don't want to stain the carpet."

"'You don't want to stain the carpet!'" Clara said mockingly.

Edgar laughed, despite not feeling much like laughing. "You are so childish sometimes."

Clara pouted, her good mood instantly ruined. "That's what Jackson used to tell me."

"Ah. I'm sorry, Clara. I didn't mean-"

"No, it's okay." She set down the wine bottle and turned off the music.

"I'm sorry," he said again.

"It's really okay. I'm sorry you've had to put up with me so much for the past week. It can't have been very fun for you, spending so much time comforting your best friend's fiancée."

"It hasn't been all bad. I just don't know how to cheer you up when I feel so lost myself. It's hard for me to even function like a normal person right now, let alone try to help someone else."

"I'm sorry. I haven't been very understanding towards you." She walked into the sitting room and sank into the couch. "I miss him so much."

"I do too. I know it's not cool for guys to be sensitive, but damn it, I miss him."

Clara smiled and then began to sob helplessly, tears splashing onto the leather couch.

"Aw. Don't cry. You're going to make me cry."

"All I ever do is cry lately," Clara said through her tears. "Do you think it will always be like this?"

"I don't know, but I really hope not. I can't take much more of this."

"How do people cope with losing a loved one, much less when it's an unexpected death? I keep wondering how differently I would feel now if he had cancer or an illness. If we had known it was coming. There would have been time to prepare."

"I don't think it would have mattered much even if we had known in advance," Edgar said. "He would still be gone and we would still be mourning the loss."

"It's not fair. It's just...how can I go on without him? He was everything to me."

"I know, Clara. Maybe grief counseling would help. Or focusing on your career and hanging out with your friends."

"My friends are already sick of me. They won't say it, but I know they hate hearing me talk about it. They wish I would move on, but they don't understand what I'm going through. I know they mean well and they try to help as much as they can, but I feel like I have to stay strong around them, so they don't see how fragile I am right now. They would just worry more if they knew how I really feel."

"I've pushed myself away from almost all of my other friends over the years," Edgar said. "Jackson was my only real friend. I'm glad I have you at least."

"At least?" Clara laughed.

"You know what I mean! It's not like we were ever close before."

"Yeah. Well, it's not like I didn't try. I always wanted us to be friends."

"Sorry. I guess that's my fault. I never expected you to stick around for so long."

"Gee thanks..."

"I'm just being honest. And it's partly the wine talking. But I never expected Jackson to find someone he cared so much about. I never imagined him settling down. He was so crazy in college. He-"

"What was he like? I didn't meet him until after college, so I always wondered what he was like back then."

"Oh God. He was always so much fun to hang out with, but you know that. He was popular, of course. He was practically guaranteed the lead role in every theatre production on campus. He liked to party a lot, so he dragged me out every weekend to random parties where I didn't know anyone. Sometimes he didn't know anyone either, but no one ever minded if he showed up. I tagged along and I was happy just to be around him." Edgar smiled slightly as he reminisced.

"There was this one time we snuck into a frat party. It was one of those parties where you're only supposed to go if you're 21, so they don't get busted for promoting underage drinking at their frat house. Anyways, it was our freshman year and Jackson was determined for us to get into the party, even though we were only 18. He had this plan for us to go in the back door when no one was paying attention. So, we get to the frat house and we're casually strolling around to the back of the house, trying to see if anyone is watching us. There was a huge guy at the front, IDing people. We get to the back and no one is there, so we thought we were good. We try opening the door and.... it's locked. Jackson suggested we try getting past the guy at the front, so we go back around and Jackson is trying everything he can to convince the guy to let us in. Finally, another guy comes out and the two of them escorted us away."

Edgar stopped for a minute and chuckled. "Jackson was so pissed off, but I was kind of relieved that was the worst that happened to us. We went back to our dorm and had an upperclassman buy us alcohol, then we sat in our tiny dorm all night, drinking beers, and watching movies. It was great," Edgar finished.

Clara had sat still almost the entire time Edgar was telling the story, entranced hearing about Jackson's past pre-Clara. "I wish I had known him then," she said somberly.

"Nah. He was fun, but he wasn't the same Jackson you knew. It took him awhile to figure things out and finally grow up a little. I was always the responsible one."

"Still. I appreciate the story. I like hearing about how he was before I met him. It's like there was this entirely different Jackson before I knew him."

Edgar was still reminiscing about the past, so he was barely paying attention to Clara anymore. "Yeah" was all he said, daydreaming about his college days.

"Ah. I should probably get to bed," Clara said suddenly, checking the time on her cellphone. "I didn't realize how late it was."

"Okay. Want me to help you clean up before I head out?"

"No, it's okay. I'll do it tomorrow. I'm really exhausted all of a sudden. I want to sleep for a few days. I wish I could sleep at all."

"I understand, trust me. Well, okay. I guess I'll see you at the funeral this weekend then." Edgar stood, grabbed the nearly empty wine bottle he had been drinking from, and headed towards the door. He put on his coat and started getting his shoes on.

"Wait," Clara said hesitantly, standing and walking to him. "Do you...do you want to stay the night?" She asked.

"Uh... what?"

"I mean. I really hate sleeping alone," she explained. "I was so used to sleeping with Jackson every night. The bed is enormous. I'm not trying to hit on you or something. I really don't want to be alone tonight."

"Well, okay. I guess it's okay." He stepped out of his shoes and hung his coat in the hall closet again.

Clara stumbled her way to the bedroom, plopping down on her side of the bed, and starting to drift off to sleep. Edgar followed her slowly, still somewhat hesitant about sleeping in the same bed as his dead best friend's fiancée.

"Are you sure you're okay with this?" He asked.

Clara mumbled an incoherent response and he climbed into bed.

"Goodnight, Clara," he said, sliding under the covers and burrowing his head into Jackson's pillow.

CHAPTER 10:
Clara

Clara had called Edgar over to comfort her. Officer Wilson had left when Clara started drinking and Clara didn't want to be alone. When he arrived, she was already well into her first bottle of wine and the effects were showing.

"Ah, I should probably stop drinking," Clara said, struggling to remain standing, and becoming more and more dizzy from the alcohol.

"You're fine," Edgar said, laughing. "You've barely had anything to drink," he said, glancing at the wine bottle.

"I haven't drunk this much in a while. I don't want to get sick," she said, setting down the bottle. "Especially if you're not going to join me. It's no fun drinking alone."

"Well, maybe I'll run to the liquor store on the corner and grab a few more bottles of wine?" He asked expectantly.

"Are you sure? You wouldn't mind?"

"No, not at all! I'll be back soon."

He headed back outside and Clara slumped to the ground in the kitchen, contemplating the decisions she had been making lately. She hadn't gone to work since Jackson died and didn't know when she would feel well enough to handle the fiasco that was going to be. She couldn't hang out much with her other friends because they were getting sick of her morose demeanor. But, should she really get drunk with Edgar? Was that the smart thing to do right now? She wondered about it for a few minutes, then decided it was worth it. She didn't want to feel so much pain anymore. She wanted to feel happy and carefree, even if it was only for a few hours. Besides, Edgar had been fun to hang out with lately. He was turning out to be a great friend. And what was the harm in two friends drinking together? She was glad she had him around to keep her company in her misery.

Edgar returned with two bottles. "I bought one red and one white. I didn't know which kind you preferred."

"Normally, white. But honestly I'll drink either right now."

She grabbed the bottle of white wine from him and opened it. "Might as well start now," she said, drinking directly from the bottle.

He followed quickly after with his own bottle of wine. Soon, they were lying on the couch and reminiscing about their favorite memories with Jackson. Edgar had known him much longer, so Clara wanted to know everything about Jackson when he was young. He didn't talk much about his past. Clara wished she had known him longer.

After no time at all, they were both drunk and clumsily

navigating their way through story after story about Jackson. Edgar spoke about their childhood and all the trouble Jackson had gotten into when he was young. He was never a particularly bad child; he just wasn't great at following rules and didn't respond well to criticism. He was the perpetual time-out child, the one who always had to stay inside during recess. He was never outright mean to other students, but his parents spoiled him immensely and had raised him in a way that made him think he was able to get everything he wanted. He didn't yet understand that he wasn't entitled to anything just because his parents thought so. As he and Edgar grew up though, Edgar taught him how to be more selfless and loving, how to respect others, and work hard to achieve success. In return, Jackson showed Edgar how to stand up for himself and to never be apologetic or ashamed of wanting to reach your goals and live out your dreams. They were perfectly complementary to each other; they balanced each other out and helped each other navigate the woes of adolescence and awkward teenage years.

***

Jackson and Edgar stood near the basketball hoop at recess. Edgar was crying because the other boys didn't want him to be on their team. He wasn't the best player and no one wanted to lose by having Edgar on their basketball team. Jackson was trying to convince Edgar they could do something else besides play basketball.

"Come on," he said. "Let's go on the swings or climb the jungle gym. I bet I can hang upside down longer than you!"

"No. I wanted to play basketball and I know that's all you

wanna do too," Edgar whined. "I'm not that bad. Why don't they want me to play with them?"

"It's okay, Edgar. They don't matter. They're dumb anyways," Jackson said, loudly enough for the other boys to hear.

Suddenly, the basketball came flying towards Jackson's face. He swiftly caught it and stared at the group of boys who had thrown it at him.

"Who threw this?" He yelled, stomping over to the group.

Edgar chased after him. "No, Jackson, it's okay! Don't do anything stupid!"

But Jackson ignored him. "I said, who threw this ball? Or are you too chicken to tell me?" He asked angrily.

The group of boys all snickered, whispering to themselves, but no one spoke up.

Jackson chucked the ball into the group and Edgar grabbed his arm, trying to hold him back. "What are you guys going to do, huh?" Jackson screamed. "Not so tough now that I'm over here. You can't leave out my friend. He's a better person than all of you losers put together."

One of the boys finally stepped forward. He was the tallest of the group and was the star of the basketball team. "Sorry, Jackson. We just don't want to do badly 'cause of him. We aren't trying to be mean."

"Well, you should have thought of that sooner!" Jackson responded, punching the tall boy in the nose.

Blood spurted out of the tall boy's nose and the boy clutched his nose, unsure of what to do. Someone else ran off to tell the teacher in charge of monitoring the playground that day and

Jackson was forced to stay in the library for an entire week of recess, as well as enduring in school suspension. Poor Edgar was left alone outside during recess, wandering aimlessly across the school grounds for the week. He would have given anything to be the one confined to the library and studying.

***

"Geez, I can't believe Jackson was like that," Clara said, astonished.

Edgar simply laughed. "Yeah, he was a wild child. I tried to keep him in check."

Clara shook her head back and forth. "Wow. He never really talked about his childhood much, so I had no idea. I mean, I knew he got into trouble a few times, but I didn't know anything specific."

"I have plenty of stories if you ever want to hear them."

"How did he act as a teenager? Did he date much? I know I was his first serious girlfriend, but what about before me? Were there...a lot of girlfriends?"

Edgar paused cautiously. Jackson had dated dozens of girls, never settling for one, always having another girl or two waiting for when he was available again. He dated carelessly. He didn't believe in love or serious relationships and couldn't begin to imagine wanting to be with someone long enough to fall in love, much less get married. Jackson tread through the dating world, never quite happy, never satisfied, until he met Clara. And even then, it had taken him six years to finally commit to her.

Meanwhile, Edgar was fine with taking Jackson's cast-offs. After dating Jackson, most girls were all too happy to jump into the arms of a soft-spoken, sensitive, romantic. Edgar dated several girls over the years, all the relationships committed, somewhat serious ones. He dated to find someone to marry, not just to date or have guaranteed sex as Jackson did. Edgar never found someone he was compatible enough with sadly and was still holding out for that special person he could spend the rest of his life with. He decided not to tell Clara the entire truth. She didn't need to know all the gory details of Jackson's dating history.

"Well, none of them were ever serious. It doesn't matter. You were the one he chose to be with, so none of those other girls are important."

"You're right. I don't know why I asked. Just sick curiosity."

"It's okay."

Edgar and Clara were both exhausted after talking for hours. They were both falling asleep on the couch, each of them curled up on opposite ends, when Clara suddenly jolted awake.

"Oh, sorry I'm falling asleep," she apologized. "I'm exhausted. I think I should go to bed and try to get a decent night of sleep."

"Probably a good idea," Edgar replied drowsily. "God I'm pretty drunk still. Do you mind if I crash here? I don't think I should drive home right now."

"Yeah, of course. I don't mind at all. I don't want you driving like this anyways," Clara said.

"Okay, thanks." Edgar stretched and yawned.

Clara began walking towards the bedroom. "Night, Edgar."

Edgar stood. "Well, actually...do you think it would be too weird if I slept in your bed with you? I'm so tired and I don't know if I'll sleep well on the couch. The bed is big enough for both of us."

Clara stared at him sleepily and drunk. "Sure, why not? We are friends, after all."

Edgar smiled. "Okay then." He followed her into the bedroom and climbed into bed with her.

Is this weird? Clara wondered as she lay in her bed with her dead fiancé's best friend. *He should probably be sleeping on the couch.* But she was too drunk to find it more than a little strange and she was far too tired to protest. Instead, she drifted off to sleep rather peacefully for the first time in several nights.

***

Clara woke up the next morning with a massive hangover. She felt around on her nightstand and thanked her drunken self from last night for leaving a glass of water and aspirin within reach. She quickly swallowed both and waited for the effects to take place. She rolled to the other side of her bed to sprawl out and try to fall asleep again but was surprised to find a body occupying Jackson's usual side of the bed. She screamed and immediately jumped out of bed. Luckily, she discovered she was still dressed in her clothes from yesterday, so at least she hadn't fallen asleep in a sheer tank top and tiny shorts like usual.

Edgar sat up. "Ow," he complained. "You rolled right over me!"

"Oh. Um. Sorry, Edgar. How did you- I mean...what happened last night?" She asked, pacing the bedroom, not quite meeting his eyes. She hadn't- oh God...she *hoped* they hadn't done anything stupid. But she couldn't remember anything after Officer Wilson had left.

"No, no, no!" He responded, automatically getting out of the bed also. "Nothing happened last night. I mean- no, nothing like that. You called me, I came over, we talked, drank *a lot* of wine...and we both cried, talking about Jackson and remembering all our great times together. You didn't want to sleep alone, so I said I would sleep on the other side of the bed. Nothing happened, I promise. I would never take advantage of you like that," he said solemnly.

"Okay. I believe you," Clara said slowly. "God, it's just...this entire week has been crazy. I don't feel like myself at all. I wouldn't be happy with myself if I had done something stupid last night." She continued to pace and Edgar grabbed her arm gently to stop her.

"I know exactly how you feel and I'm here for you," he said.

"Thank you, Edgar. I appreciate everything you've done. I don't know what I would have done without you to talk to. You're the only person who really gets it."

"I know. You've helped me a lot too, I promise," Edgar replied.

"Shit. Officer Wilson is coming back at 3 today. She was asking me so many things I don't know the answers to. Like, about Jackson's finances and his bank statements. We never discussed our finances seriously because I just assumed we would before we were married, so I'm not sure what to tell her."

"Just be honest," Edgar said simply. "Honesty is always the best route. Besides, I'm sure Officer Wilson knows you weren't the one who killed him. There's no evidence that would support that theory," he said comfortingly.

"You're right. But it doesn't make it any less terrifying being a suspect for a murder case and getting interrogated with the same questions repeatedly. Have the police talked to you yet?"

"No, but I'm sure they will soon. It's not like Jackson had many people he was close to, so I'm probably their next suspect."

"Ugh. I want this whole thing to be over," Clara moaned. "This is such a nightmare."

"I know. Once they find the murderer and he or she has been arrested, things will start to calm down. We have to stay hopeful until then."

"What if they can't figure out who did it?" Clara asked anxiously. "What if there isn't enough evidence to prove who switched the guns? Then what?"

"I don't know. But whoever it is, I hope they catch them."

CHAPTER 11:
Edgar

Idon't understand how he was paying all his bills and living such a comfortable lifestyle if he didn't have the money. When Officer Wilson showed me Jackson's bank statements, I was completely taken off guard. You didn't know about this, did you?" Clara asked Edgar as they sat on opposite sides of a bistro table, sipping coffee, her with a mocha and he with black coffee.

"Actually, there's something I've been meaning to tell you." Edgar ruffled his dark shaggy hair and scrunched up his face, like he always did when he was nervous.

"So, you did know about it?"

"I've been loaning Jackson money."

"For what?" Clara asked in astonishment. "There's no reason why he would need financial help!"

"Jackson was never smart with his money. His parents cut him off from his inheritance once he was out of college."

"But he's their favorite child. That makes no sense..."

"I know, but that's what they decided. Anyways, ever since he was young, he's always been financially irresponsible. He never learned how to manage his money or set a budget for himself. At his first job, the second he got paid he would go out and blow half of his money on beer and video games. I'm telling you all of this because I've been helping him for a while now. He didn't want anyone to know because he was embarrassed that he was in so deep." Edgar sipped his coffee thoughtfully.

"How much have you been loaning to him? How long has this been going on? I can't believe he didn't tell me...I could have helped him work things out."

"Don't feel bad, Clara. I'm his oldest friend. He didn't want you to know because he was trying to protect you. He didn't want you to think less of him. I'm sure he would have told you before the wedding."

"How long have you been loaning him money, Edgar? And how exactly do you have all this extra money lying around? I know you have a decent role on the show, but I also know Jackson is the highest paid actor on *Dispatching David*."

"It's been... oh God, at least three years, I think, since he first approached me for help. Unlike Jackson, I've built up a rather large savings account over the years. I was preparing for an emergency, my retirement, my future. I don't have a significant other or kids and I don't live a particularly extravagant lifestyle. It was okay for me to dip into my savings and help out my best friend."

Clara finished her mocha and stood to throw it away. She tightened her scarf around her neck and zipped up her heavy coat.

"Well, this has been immensely enlightening," she said, heading towards the door of the coffee shop. "Thanks for filling me in, Edgar," Clara said angrily, stalking outside the coffee shop and letting the door slam shut so that the holiday bells jingled obnoxiously above it.

Edgar calmly stayed in his seat and waved goodbye as Clara walked past the window. She scoffed and quickened her pace. She was upset now, but soon enough she would realize that he had only been looking out for Jackson. Without his help, Jackson wouldn't have been able to afford all the things Clara had so desperately claimed she couldn't live without. Really, Edgar had saved their relationship. He knew Clara pretended not to care about money, but it was all too obvious that she expected certain things and was not willing to settle for less than what she felt she deserved.

Edgar stayed at the coffee shop, contemplating his life and all the events that had led up to this moment. He really had been the best friend he could to Jackson. He had stayed by his side when many lesser men would have faltered. Why couldn't Clara see that? He wasn't selfish and he hadn't told her about the money sooner because he respected Jackson too much to reveal his secrets. Now that he was dead, however, Edgar felt all the secrets threatening to spill out of him one by one.

CHAPTER 12:
Jackson

Jackson steeled himself and tried to work up the courage to ask Edgar for money. He was running out of options and Edgar was the only hope he had left.

"Edgar, I have a favor to ask of you. But please hear me out before shooting me down."

"Okay," Edgar said cautiously, wary as he always was when Jackson needed a favor.

"You're my last chance of being able to stay in this apartment and continue living the lifestyle I've become used to." He took a deep breath and continued nervously. "This is really embarrassing to talk about and I hope you understand that I don't want anyone else to know."

"Not even Clara? Or your parents?" Edgar asked, suspiciously. What did Jackson need help with that he didn't want his girlfriend or parents knowing about?

"No, not even them. I... I've gotten myself into a lot of debt. And when I say a lot, I mean, hundreds of thousands. It could even be millions at this point. I honestly don't know. There's no way I can even begin to pay it off and well, my savings account is almost nonexistent at this point. I don't know who else to turn to and you're one of the only people I trust. I would really appreciate the help, Edgar."

"Okay, I'll do it," Edgar said, quietly. "I'll help you. Just let me know how much you need and we can work something out."

Jackson stared at him. "Are you sure? You don't want to ask more questions or know more about the situation before you agree to this?"

"Well...okay. How did you get into so much debt?" He asked.

"Ugh, man, I hate talking about this. I'm such a fucking moron. It's partly because of the cars. The apartment is too expensive, even with how much I make. Clara expects extravagant dinners and gifts all the time. I guess I never learned how to manage my money well enough. I didn't pay much attention to my bank account because I was making so much money. By the time I looked at my bank statement, I had almost spent every dollar I had. This would ruin me if anyone found out," Jackson said, looking down at his hands folded on his lap. "Please, Edgar- I don't want anyone to find out."

They were at a coffee shop close to Edgar's apartment and were sitting at a quiet table in the corner. Barely any other customers were around because the weather was so crummy outside. Over a foot of snow, icy roads, and powerful gusts of wind in NYC made it a day for staying at home.

Edgar looked at Jackson while he wasn't paying attention. He saw his best friend, really his only friend, how worried he was, and how much he needed him. He wasn't going to let him down. He never had and now was not the time to start, even though Edgar knew if Jackson was really in that much debt it had to be because of something worse than too many nice dinners or buying one too many luxury cars. He knew Jackson was irresponsible, but there had to be something else going on. What had he done? "Of course I'll help you. Just let me know how much you need, man. I won't tell anyone; don't worry."

"Seriously? Thank you, Edgar! Oh my God, you're the best," Jackson exhaled loudly, a sigh of relief. "I promise I'll pay you back when I can and you can tack on interest or whatever you want if it takes me awhile to get the money."

"It's fine. Don't worry about paying me back. I'm happy I can help you out," Edgar responded, mostly because he was so flattered that Jackson had asked him out of everyone he knew. He was the one Jackson chose: over his parents, his other friends, his sister, and... Clara.

He was honored that Jackson trusted him so much, but he couldn't help but wonder if something else was going on, something he didn't want anyone to know about. He had witnessed firsthand Jackson's financial irresponsibility for almost their entire lives. Edgar wondered what Jackson's real secret was or if he was simply imagining something more sinister.

CHAPTER 13:
Clara

It was the day of Jackson's funeral at last. Clara was thankful because it meant Jackson's parents would finally be returning to Minneapolis the next day. It was a gratifying thought, but somehow still sad. She wanted to get along with his parents and it wasn't because of a lack of effort on her part. She had tried everything the past six years to get along with them. They simply wouldn't budge. At this point, there was no use in trying anymore. She supposed that after today she wouldn't have a reason to see them again.

Jackson's younger sister had arrived earlier in the day. They all went out for breakfast, where Jessica was berated by her parents for showing up the day of the funeral. They claimed she didn't care enough and said Jessica was probably happy he was gone, so the focus could be on her. Of course, this was ridiculous; Jessica was as devastated as everyone else about Jackson's death. Just because she had never been particularly close to her brother, that didn't mean she wished ill upon him. Besides, she had a busy work schedule and it had been nearly impossible for her to get a few days off to fly to NYC.

Thousands of people showed up at Jackson's funeral. His parents had expected a large crowd, but they weren't prepared for this. Long lines of people saying how sorry they were and bombarding them with sympathy cards and bouquets of ugly flowers. It was all so absurd. All they wanted was for their son to come back and no amount of people or apologies or gifts could ever make up for that loss. During the funeral service, Rick read a heartwarming Bible passage. Jessica sang an original song about grief that made almost all the funeralgoers cry. Clara stood at the podium and recited an E.E. Cummings poem titled "I carry your heart," which they had planned to use as a reading at their wedding. How ironic now to use it at a celebration to honor the dead, instead of its original intent of honoring the joyous ceremony of two lives becoming one.

It wasn't an entirely awful day for Clara though. She blossomed under the crowd's ravenous attention. She liked that people thought her reading of the poem was touching and that everyone cared how she was holding up, or at least they pretended to care. She loved the flowers in multicolored vases scattered throughout her apartment and the baked goods and home cooked meals people brought over nearly every day. The only thing she didn't like was hearing everyone talk about Jackson as if he had been their closest friend. "Oh, Clara, Jackson was a great guy!" They would say. Or "It's so awful. He was so young. He had his whole life ahead of him. It's a shame you two weren't able to get married." That hurt the most. Clara had missed out on her future with Jackson before she ever had a chance to fully appreciate the promise, the possibilities, the untold joy of being married to her soulmate. Now she was sentenced to a lifetime of loneliness and bitterness, daydreaming over what could have been. Clara didn't plan on ever dating or marrying anyone else. Jackson had been the one for her and she wanted to honor him by keeping the promise they had made to each other when they agreed to get married. Maybe she would adopt a child or move back to Michigan to live near her family again. Maybe this was her chance to embark on a career she cared about. To travel the world and experience different cultures, so she could appreciate her own life once again. Maybe she would grow from the experience and it would help her grasp a deeper understanding of human nature. But then again, maybe not.

Jackson's parents hovered near the entrance, Susan weeping uncontrollably while Rick tried futilely to comfort her. Eventually, they joined her near the food, where they all forced themselves to eat despite their lack of appetite. Jackson's sister, Jessica, walked over cautiously, knowing her parents were probably going to bitch her out for something stupid. Jessica was dressed in a flouncy black blazer with charcoal pants and sky-high heels. Her auburn curls were tousled to perfection and she didn't look as if she was suitably dressed for a funeral.

"Hey, Clara. The service was beautiful," Jessica said, hugging Clara.

"I tried my best. I wanted everything about this day to honor Jackson."

"I know." Jessica sighed. "I regret not spending more time with Jackson. I guess this is what happens when you don't get to say goodbye to someone you love."

"Yeah," Clara responded, straightening her sleeveless black dress she had recently purchased from Ralph Lauren. "I know we all wish we had more time with him."

"It's weird to think I'm an only child now. I don't know what to tell people when they ask about my siblings. 'Oh yeah, I had a brother, but he was shot while filming a TV show where he acted as the lead role.' What am I supposed to say?"

Jackson and Jessica's parents looked as if they were going to strangle Jessica from their fury.

"Jessica, now is most definitely not the time. You are being rather disrespectful about your brother and your mother can barely stand to look at you right now," Rick said in a hushed tone, trying not to raise any unwanted attention from the other funeralgoers.

"Well, I'm sorry you guys are mourning, but I lost my brother. It doesn't matter if I didn't see him all the time or if we were never close, he was still my brother."

"Oh, Jessica. Silly child. Of course you're mourning too. I wasn't trying to imply that at all. I don't know where you would get an idea like that. I would be more worried if you weren't upset, but clearly you are."

"Good to know you see that I'm mourning..." Jessica said, whipping out a flask from her purse. "Anyone else want some?" She asked, holding it out and shaking it in her hand.

"Jessica!" Her mom exclaimed. "How dare you bring that foul substance in here! Put that away right now!"

Jessica swigged a liquid from the flask and laughed viciously. "You guys never did understand me," she said, walking away while sipping intermittently from the flask.

"She doesn't know how to act properly in public," Susan said, sighing and exchanging a look with Rick. "I tried my best to teach her, but there was only so much I could do raising a girl like her."

"It's okay. Everyone mourns in their own way," Clara said quietly.

Rick snorted and put his arm around Susan. "Indeed."

Susan rested her head on Rick's shoulder and sighed dramatically. "At least Jessica showed up. I'll be glad when this is over and we can go home."

"I agree, darling. Soon enough," Rick responded, squeezing her shoulder in comfort.

"I think I'm going to go talk to more people," Clara said.

"Alright, dear. It was nice seeing you again. You look lovely." Susan said, smiling.

"Thanks..." Clara responded, walking away gratefully.

She couldn't handle being around Jackson's parents for another second, especially if they were going to talk so rudely about their only remaining child. She left to find Jessica and spotted her by the entrance of the church, sitting on a bench outside.

"It's so cold out here. Want to come back inside?" Clara said, visibly shivering.

"Nah, I'd rather be outside and freeze to death than spend any more time listening to my parents," Jessica remarked.

Clara sat next to her on the bench and wrapped her arms

around her body, trying to stay warm. "I wanted to make sure you were okay. Your parents can be pretty, um..."

"Rude? Mean? Bitchy?" Jessica said with a slightly sarcastic laugh.

"Yeah, well... How are you?"

"I'm- I don't know. I wish I could have told him I love him. And how proud I am of him for everything he's accomplished. And...so many other things."

"He knew you loved him. He never spoke badly about you, Jessica. You weren't close, but it's not as if you hated each other."

"I know. I just wish things had ended differently."

"I think we all do."

"Right."

Jessica shifted on the bench, tucking the flask away in her purse.

"Is that really alcohol in there?" Clara asked hesitantly.

Jessica threw back her head and laughed heartily. "No, it's hot tea."

Clara giggled despite her best efforts to hold it back. "Sorry about your parents. They're just upset."

Jessica's smile stopped and she pursed her lips. "They could at least pretend to care about me. They act like they lost their only child. I know he was their favorite; it's not like they ever kept it a secret. They did everything for him and left me to fend for myself. But Jackson is the one who's gone and I'm still here, so they could at least pretend they give a shit about me."

"It's not really fair, but if it makes you feel any better, they've never treated me well either."

Jessica smiled. "I know. You don't deserve that either. I've always liked you. I wanted to see you and Jackson get married and have kids, so I could have a couple of nieces and nephews. That would have been nice."

"Thanks."

Jessica put her arm around Clara's shoulder and squeezed. "Well, it's pretty fucking cold out here. What do you think; should we leave? Have we stayed long enough?"

Clara nodded. "I think so."

They both stood and walked to Clara's car across the parking lot. Clara had driven them to the funeral and she had planned on bringing Jessica to the airport before she left, but they still had a few hours of time to kill.

"My flight doesn't leave until five. Do you want to do something before you bring me to the airport? I hate being there early and waiting around to board the plane."

Clara paused for a moment in reflective thought. "Sure. There's this amazing coffee shop we can go to. Jackson and I used to go there all the time."

"That sounds great. I'm a big fan of coffee," Jessica said, rubbing her arms to try to stop goosebumps from forming.

"Jackson drank his black and it always disgusted me," Clara said.

"I know! Who enjoys the taste of black coffee? He is so weird! I mean, he *was*...so...weird," she corrected herself.

The two women sat in silence during the rest of the drive to the coffee shop, each contemplating the loss of the man they had both loved. When they arrived at the coffee shop, they ordered and sat near the gas fireplace, each woman struggling desperately to feel warm again.

CHAPTER 14:
Edgar

Look, I know I said I would help you, but I didn't think it would be for this long, Jackson. I thought it was going to be for a few months until you could save enough money to start paying down your debt," Edgar said.

"Please don't be mad, Edgar. I can't stand it if you're mad at me," Jackson said, his big brown eyes wide, appealing to Edgar's sensitive nature.

"Jackson...I can't do this forever. I have a lot of money saved, but I had it saved for an emergency, for my future, for retirement."

"I know. I'm sorry. It will only be a little bit longer, I promise. I need more time though."

Edgar ran his hands through his shaggy hair and adjusted his glasses. "Okay, fine. But, don't you think you should move to a less expensive apartment and stop going out all the time? It's going to take longer to get your finances in order if you don't cut back on your spending."

"I'm fine, I swear. I barely spend any money lately. Besides, I don't want to move. What would Clara think? She would panic if she thought I didn't have any money left. She isn't superficial, but I know she likes the money."

"I know, but...I really think you should at least tell her that money is a little tight, so she is aware you're having financial issues. You don't have to tell her everything, but then you won't have to keep up the charade anymore. I'm sure she will understand."

"You don't get it," Jackson said, shaking his head and biting his lip. "I have a reputation. I can't let anyone know I'm struggling. You can't even begin to imagine how embarrassing that would be for me, Edgar. I'm supposed to be a wealthy TV actor; I have an image to maintain. Everyone would be so judgmental. Clara would leave me if she knew the truth, not to mention how my parents would react if they knew what was going on. And I can't even begin to imagine how my fans would react. I can't let them down."

"Clara doesn't just want you for your money."

"No, but she wants someone who is well-off and financially stable, and I don't blame her. She deserves that."

"You're being ridiculous. This is the last payment I'll give you, Jackson."

Edgar pulled a blank check from his wallet and passed it across the table discretely. "Just try to keep the amount lower this time."

They were at their usual coffee shop, so Jackson could get his caffeine fix for the day. Jackson smiled and swept the check into his hand, placing it in his pocket.

"It's the last time, I promise," Jackson said earnestly. "Thanks, Edgar. You're the best friend a guy could have."

CHAPTER 15:
Clara

After the funeral, Clara still didn't feel as if she had any closure. She knew she wouldn't feel better until Jackson's murderer had been caught. She felt as if she was in an awful dream, trudging through each day doing the bare minimum to survive. She hadn't been to work all week. She hadn't even called in after the first day she had taken off. Her boss and co-workers had been understanding so far, but she wondered when they would begin to protest her absence. But honestly, she didn't care. Let them fire her. She could find another job. Or not. It didn't matter much either way. Nothing mattered anymore.

Officer Wilson would be arriving at her apartment soon. Clara had asked to reschedule their meeting because she felt too stressed from planning the funeral and making sure everything was in order. She had dropped off Jessica at the airport and Jackson's parents were finally gone as well, so she was back to moping around alone in her apartment. She straightened up the sitting room, fluffing pillows and dusting the 70-inch 4K TV Jackson had insisted was necessary. Clara often found herself in a cleaning frenzy when she was stressed and anxious. This was an extreme circumstance, so the apartment had remained spotless all week.

There was a knock on the door and Clara nervously went to answer it, smoothing down her blonde hair and straightening her form-fitting, knee-length skirt.

"Hello, Clara. How are you today?" Officer Wilson greeted her.

"I'm okay. How are you?"

"Fine. May I come in?"

"Yeah, we can go into the sitting room to talk."

Officer Wilson looked around the apartment surreptitiously. "The funeral was yesterday," she remarked offhandedly.

"Yeah. Jackson's parents and sister flew in from Minnesota," Clara said. "It was a beautiful service."

Officer Wilson nodded. "That's good to hear. Well, let's get down to it. We interrogated Edgar and there is no evidence to point to him being a suspect in the case."

"That's good," Clara responded, thinking that was an obvious conclusion.

"There is, however, new evidence that makes you a more prevalent suspect."

"What?" Clara asked, wide-eyed, and sitting up straighter. "What evidence is that?"

"We discovered a receipt in your apartment for the exact type of bullets that were loaded into the gun and used to shoot Jackson."

"That's ridiculous! I don't know anything about guns or bullets! I've never even touched a gun."

"The evidence says otherwise. It's not enough to put you away yet, but we're working on it. I wanted to ask you again. Clara, did you load the gun that killed Jackson?"

"Of course not! I don't even know how to load a gun. Besides, Jackson was my fiancé. I love him more than anything in this world. Why would I want to kill him? We were supposed to get married next spring…"

"Maybe you were disappointed when you found out his money was running out."

"I told you already, Officer Wilson. I didn't know about his financial troubles. He never told me he was in debt."

"I'm sure we can find a motive if the money wasn't the reason; there are plenty of other reasons you could have wanted him dead. Maybe he wasn't paying enough attention to you. Maybe he was abusive or he cheated on you and you wanted revenge. There is always a reason. And we will figure it out, Clara. I won't stop until I've solved this case. So, if you planted the gun that killed your fiancé, it's far better if you admit it now."

"I didn't want Jackson to die! He was never abusive and he never cheated on me. We had our issues, but nothing we couldn't have fixed if we had the chance. What if someone is trying to frame me?"

"If someone is trying to frame you, then we will find out."

"How do you plan on doing that? You're already fucking up this case if you think I killed Jackson!"

"Clara, please, calm down. We don't have enough evidence to

prove anything yet. You're not going to prison. But I wouldn't try leaving the city anytime soon. If someone is trying to frame you for Jackson's death, then it's possible that they are coming after you next."

"Oh my God. What am I supposed to do? Can't you protect me?"

"We can have someone watch you, but we are short staffed right now, so it won't be a constant surveillance. It's the best we can do. We have other cases to work on and other duties besides this case."

"I understand that, but...I'm scared. And I don't want to die."

"We will do everything we can to ensure your safety," Officer Wilson said solemnly, awkwardly patting Clara on the shoulder. "I can promise you that."

"Okay. Thank you." Clara choked back a sob. She didn't want to fall apart in front of Officer Wilson yet again.

"It will be okay, Clara. I don't believe it was you."

"You don't? Then why are you interrogating me? Please help me," she begged.

"I will do my best. I have to return to the police station now. We have several other suspects to interrogate."

"Who?"

"I can't reveal that information right now since the case is ongoing, but as soon as their interrogations are over and information has been fact-checked and verified, I can let you know if we have any further leads."

"Who would want to kill Jackson? I keep asking myself this question. Who hated him so much that they wanted him to die? I just don't understand how Jackson could have done anything bad enough that someone would kill him." Clara said, her eyes filling with tears despite her best attempt to stop them.

"I have some ideas. I don't want to say anything in case I'm mistaken, but I'll be in touch soon, okay?"

Officer Wilson left the apartment, seeming like she was in a rush to get out of there. Clara hoped Officer Wilson believed she was telling the truth about Jackson. How had the police found a receipt for the bullets in their apartment? Who would have planted that on her and how had the police found the receipt? There were too many confusing questions left unanswered and Clara felt uneasy and mildly sick. She didn't want to go to prison. She didn't want Jackson to be dead. She didn't want any of this.

The Long Shadow on the Stage

CHAPTER 16:
Edgar

Jackson and Edgar were working out at a gym they often went to together. They were both in shape and maintained a healthy lifestyle. They worked out together several times a week because it was always more enjoyable to work out when you weren't alone. Jackson liked lifting weights and Edgar always spotted him. Edgar preferred riding the exercise bike or running on the treadmill. Unlike Jackson, Edgar didn't care as much about gaining muscle; he just liked staying active and spending time with his best friend.

Edgar stood beside Jackson and watched as Jackson lifted the heavy weights above his head. Jackson had tossed his shirt onto the ground beside the bench after a while; he always became sweaty while working out, no matter how long he was exercising. Jackson's muscles on his chest and arms bulged as he lifted the weights again. Edgar stared. Jackson lifted once more, but he was becoming tired and nearly dropped the weights on his face because

Edgar wasn't paying attention enough to help him out.

Jackson angrily jumped up from the weight bench. "What were you doing, Edgar? I could have crushed my skull!"

"Sorry! I- I wasn't paying attention."

"Well, what were you doing that was so captivating?" He demanded.

"Just spacing out. Sorry. I didn't mean to."

"God, Edgar. If you're going to be like that, I'll have someone else spot me next time. Just stick to your treadmill."

Edgar watched Jackson pick up his gray t-shirt from the floor and put it back on, covering his chiseled body. He looked away hastily, grabbing his water bottle and chugging most of it to look busy.

"Don't have someone else spot you. The main reason I'm motivated enough to work out is because I'm with you."

"We'll see," Jackson said. "I don't want to die from weights falling on me."

Edgar followed Jackson into the locker room and they went into shower stalls. Edgar didn't like showering at the gym because he was shy about being naked in front of other guys, but Jackson always felt gross right after working out, and didn't like going home while he was still sweaty and smelly. Edgar quickly washed his body and hopped out of the shower stall, reaching for his clothes. Jackson stood in the locker room, already in his boxers, and pulling on his jeans. Edgar finished getting dressed and shook his head back and forth, trying to stay focused. It was too late now to tell anyone. It was too late to do anything about it. It was better to keep living the way he had been. Things would work out somehow.

"You ready, man?" Jackson asked, ruffling his short, dark hair with a towel.

"Yeah, sure."

"I have a date with Clara tonight," Jackson said excitedly, his mood clearly perking up.

"Oh yeah? What are you guys going to do?"

"Probably go out to dinner or something. I don't know. I hate planning dates."

"What will you do after dinner? You could take a walk around Central Park at night. It's beautiful when it's all lit up around Christmas."

"Oh, Edgar," Jackson said, laughing. "You're such a romantic! It's a shame the ladies don't know that. You would have them crawling to you by the dozens if you weren't so damn shy."

"You know I don't care about that. I'm fine being by myself."

"Yeah, yeah. I've heard it all before. Are you sure you don't want to go out with Clara's friend, Madison? She's pretty cute and she has a great ass. Plus, I heard she's great in bed," Jackson said, winking.

"How did you hear that?" Edgar asked innocently.

"Oh, you know. Just through the grapevine. So, what do you think, a double date next weekend?"

"I don't think so. I appreciate that you're trying to hook me up, but I promise I'm happy. I don't need a relationship right now. Besides, if I wanted to date someone, it's not like I couldn't win someone over without your help."

"Okay, Edgar. Whatever you say! If you change your mind,

you know where to find me," Jackson teased, exiting the gym.

"Have fun on your date with Clara!" Edgar called after him.

"Oh, I will. I can promise you that!" Jackson yelled back, walking off into the night.

CHAPTER 17:
Edgar

Rehearsal was strange without Jackson. When they first returned to filming, everyone crowded around him, asking how he was holding up, pretending to care about his wellbeing, but mostly trying to convince him to reveal information about Jackson's death. The other cast and crew members assumed that because he was Jackson's best friend, he was in the know about the ongoing investigation. He fended off their questions and eventually they gave up. Edgar had no one to talk to or joke around with, no one to eat lunch with, or run lines with in between scenes or after rehearsal was over. He didn't have anyone to talk to about the show or someone who understood his complaints about Gus. He was happy about playing the role of David on the show, but it wasn't the same without Jackson.

"That was awful!" Gus yelled, practically tearing out his hair in frustration, and stomping towards him on the set.

"Sorry, Gus. I'm trying. I'm not used to seeing the show from a different character's perspective."

"I don't care what you're used to! You're an actor making an exorbitant amount of money per episode. You don't get the luxury of making up excuses! You're here to do a job and I expect you to do it well. Now get your shit together before I decide to cancel filming the remainder of the show," Gus threatened.

"I will, I promise. Next time will be better," Edgar said hopefully.

"Ah, what the hell. Take a break, you miscreants! I expect the scene to be twice as good when you return."

"I'll make sure it is!" Edgar swallowed nervously and hurriedly grabbed his script to reenact the scene on his own as the other actors and crew members exited the building, relieved for a break.

Edgar walked through the scene several times, his stomach grumbling at the thought of food. He hadn't eaten all day, but knew it was smarter to work through his hunger to perfect his lines and his persona. Something was missing from David's character. He had to figure out how to fix it before he became too discouraged. People started filing back into the room and Edgar checked the time in dismay. He didn't feel ready to jump back into rehearsal yet. As he was going through the scene one last time, with the actors and crew members now watching him, Gus entered the room and Edgar stopped mid-scene.

"Well, what are you doing? Why the hell did you stop? Let's see what you've been working on for the past hour."

"Uh, okay," Edgar said anxiously, setting his script down on an empty chair and walking back onto the stage. Normally he was confident in his acting abilities, but Gus was so terrifying when he was completely focused on him, so it made him lose all his confidence. He breathed in deeply a few times, trying to calm himself.

"We haven't got all day. Get your shit together or leave."

Edgar stared out into the space across the room, immersing himself into David. This scene was a monologue, one of the defining moments of the show and one of the last scenes, so it had to be perfect.

"So, I slept with my best friend's wife and he hates me now. Why does it matter? He never gave a shit about her anyways. I've watched him with her all these years and I know he never loved her. Meanwhile, here I am, alone and desperate to feel something again. I could love her if I had the chance. I just- I never had the chance." He paused, staring off again. He ran his hands through his long hair and tugged on it. "Why is it that the good guys never get the girl? It doesn't seem fair. He has everything, but he doesn't appreciate any of it. He doesn't deserve to be with her. I do. I deserve to be happy, damn it!" He paused again, this time falling to his knees on the fake hardwood floors, his head downward, his shoulders shaking as he lost control, real tears splashing onto the floor. "I can't do this anymore. It's not worth it. If I can't have happiness, then there's no point in going on. I don't want to if-" He stopped, sobs wrenching his body; he wrapped his arms around himself and rocked back and forth in pain. He pulled a pocketknife out of the pocket of his jeans, unfolded it, and held it to his wrist, the blade glistening under the glare of the lights. "It would be so easy. All I have to do is give in."

He pressed the blade to his wrist and every single person in the room was waiting in anticipation to see what would happen next. They all knew of course, but it seemed so real suddenly. The lights went off, the camera stopped rolling, and Gus stood, clapping as he walked towards Edgar.

"That was beautiful! That's what I've been waiting for, princess!" He exclaimed, clapping Edgar on the back excitedly.

Edgar smiled cautiously. "Did you film it? Was it good enough for the show?"

Gus laughed heartily. "It will do, I suppose. I had the camera crew filming just in case something usable was in there. Now we just have the final scene left." Gus turned to face the other cast and crew members in the room. "As you all know, we had a tragic accident last time we tried to film the last episode of our show. I know I can be a hardass sometimes-"

To which everyone either held back laughter or rolled their eyes.

"But I would like to think of us as a family. And I don't take kindly to any of my family members being hurt. So, before you all come into the building, there will be security guards checking everyone's bags, jackets, etc. for weapons of any kind just like there was today. I know the police have interrogated everyone here, along with several other people outside of the cast and crew, but they still haven't solved the case. We are taking every precaution necessary to ensure nothing like that horrible accident ever happens again. Don't be stupid and think you will get away with this if it was one of you who did it. The police are doing everything they can to find out who is responsible for Jackson's death. We lost a valuable member of our cast that day. Jackson Birkman was one of the good ones. Not only was he a talented and well-respected actor, but he was also engaged to a beautiful woman. He had it all. I would like to take a moment of silence to remember Jackson." He bowed his head respectfully and everyone else obeyed, each person thinking about Jackson in their own way.

Edgar stood with his head down, looking at the ground the longest. Everyone stared at him, waiting for him to come back to reality.

"It's okay," Gus said, patting him on the shoulder awkwardly. "We all loved Jackson and we all miss him."

Edgar nodded, swallowing hard, trying to compose himself. He hadn't imagined Gus would say anything to honor Jackson, so the unexpected show of sentiment was making him emotional. 'Thanks, Gus."

"Don't get the wrong idea. I'm not going soft!" Gus suddenly yelled. "We will finish the last scene tomorrow. Get some rest everyone! And get the hell out of here!" Gus said in his booming voice.

Edgar packed up his things, but Gus stopped him before he could leave.

"Whoa, whoa, princess. I need to talk to you."

"Okay. About what?" Edgar asked with trepidation. It had been a long day and he couldn't wait to go home to relax and finally eat something.

"About your scene today. That was nearly perfect! A real tearjerker. Do you think you can keep that up for tomorrow too?"

"I plan on it."

Gus chuckled and slapped him on the back hard. "Alrighty. Good. I expect nothing short of excellence then."

"I'll try my best, Gus," Edgar said with a smile.

"Keep it up and you might be landing a certain role in a movie with a certain actress named Anne Hathaway as your co-star."

"Seriously?" Edgar asked, wide-eyed in disbelief.

Gus nodded slowly. "Only the best for my star pupils. Now get some shut-eye, Sleeping Beauty. We need you at the top of your game for the final scene."

"I know. I've been working on it all week. I think I finally nailed it."

"Ah, get the hell out of here, princess. I'm sick of your face."

Edgar hid a smile. "Okay. Goodnight, Gus."

Gus waved him off disdainfully.

Edgar left the TV set with a genuine smile, feeling rather proud of himself for the day's accomplishments. He had managed to get a compliment from Gus, he was possibly going to be in a movie with Anne Hathaway whom he completely idolized, and after tomorrow he would be done dealing with Gus forever.

Edgar felt as if he was finally where he was meant to be. He owned the stage in a way no man before him ever had. He was going to make the ending of *Dispatching David* the most memorable ending of a TV show in history. He had just finished the next to last rehearsal. If everything went according to plan, tomorrow would be the last day of filming the show. Then, the episode would air and millions of adoring fans would praise him as the one who had saved the show. He still mourned Jackson's death; it hadn't been long and he knew it would take years to recover from the loss of his best friend, if he ever did. But he also knew Jackson had always cared about his happiness and right now playing David on a popular TV show was bringing him the greatest joy he had ever known. One of the extras had stepped in to fill Edgar's old role and it was a little strange to adjust to acting in the scene from a different character's perspective, especially after years of playing a different role on the show. But now he was in the flow of things. He felt more respected than before. Previously, he had just been another actor on the show, but now, now he was the star. Everyone else onstage revolved around him. Everything David said and did had a weight ten times that of any other character. Most people watched the show just to see what new crazy thing David would do that week and even though he was a dick most of the time, his character had a few redeeming qualities to make him likeable enough to the audience, so they cared about what happened to him. And that was important; in fact, it was key to the show because of how it was supposed to end. The ending would be the greatest ending of a TV show in their lifetime. The ending was supposed to be perfect because that's the part everyone remembers. The ending of a TV show is the part fans obsess over for years and years after the show has stopped creating new episodes. It's the thing people dissect until they have torn it to shreds, trying to figure out every detail and come up with explanations for each action of the characters. A good ending will satisfy the fans, but a great ending will be remembered and revered forever.

CHAPTER 18:
Clara

Clara wondered if she should go to therapy. She needed to talk to someone that wasn't so close to the situation. The only person she really had was Edgar and he was probably growing sick of her constantly talking about Jackson. Besides, even if he wasn't becoming annoyed, wasn't it far healthier if they both stopped dwelling on the past and continuously sharing their memories of Jackson in some sick show to prove who had known him better? Maybe she would call a psychiatrist. Or maybe she needed medication to deter her constant depression that had set on after his death. Or maybe she simply needed to find a productive way to spend her time: volunteering, helping at charity functions, teaching underprivileged children how to read. None of these seemed like the greatest idea and she didn't know if any of those things would help her feel better. All she knew was that something needed to change if she was ever going to be able to pick up the pieces of her life and be happy again.

She powered on her laptop and began scrolling through the pages on Google listing things to do in the area. There were dozens of ways she could spend her time, if only something would jump out at her. She spotted an ad for The Humane Society. Several dozen puppies and kittens needed to be adopted. Clara hadn't considered owning a pet, but it would be comforting and she would be saving the life of a helpless animal that would otherwise endure an unfortunate life in a cage. Or worse, have its life cut short if no one adopted it. She grabbed her purse and coat, hurrying out the door before she could change her mind. Today was the day she was going to adopt a kitten.

Clara came home several hours later with an adorable gray kitten with blue eyes. She decided to name him Henry. Henry was so tiny and stayed cozily curled up in her lap while she sat on the couch watching TV. She petted him softly and he purred at her touch, snuggling against her happily. She had stopped by the pet store to buy cat food, water and food dishes, several toys, and a fuzzy leopard print cat bed. She smiled to herself as she watched "Property Brothers" reruns all afternoon. Clara had unconditional love and that was the greatest thing she could hope for now.

CHAPTER 19: Officer Wilson

Officer Wilson was on her way to the store where the bullets had been purchased that had resulted in Jackson's death. It was a sporting goods store in Queens. According to Google Maps, it was a 25-minute drive from the NYPD 19th Precinct, which meant much longer in NY traffic. Officer Wilson was going to try to find the cashier who had rang up the purchase and see if they remembered who had bought the bullets. She knew it was a long shot, but hopefully an employee could shed some light on the situation. She walked into the store and went straight to the customer service desk.

"Hi, I'm Officer Wilson," she said, brandishing her police badge as proof of her status. "I'm working on a case involving the death of Jackson Birkman. We found this receipt with a suspect who possibly caused his death and I wanted to verify the purchaser. Is there any way I can talk to the cashier who rang up the bullets?"

She pulled out the receipt and peered at the cashier's name on it. "It says on the receipt that an employee named Denise was the cashier?"

The customer service representative dialed a number on the phone perched on the desk and several minutes later a young woman appeared at the customer service desk.

"Yeah?" Denise said, standing with a hand on her hip and loudly smacking her gum.

"Hi, two weeks ago a customer came through your lane and purchased a 40 S&W cartridge for a GLOCK 22 that resulted in someone's death." Officer Wilson held up the receipt. "Do you remember who the customer was? Any identifying details about them? It was on November 7th around 2:30 pm."

Denise grabbed the receipt from her hand and read the information on it. She shook her head. "Nope. I don't remember no one like that. I have dozens of customers every single day. How can you expect me to remember one person out of all them?"

Officer Wilson clenched her teeth and took the receipt back, placing it in the safety of her binder. "Are you sure? No one suspicious came through your lane? Nothing out of the ordinary happened that day?"

"Nah. Nothing like that. Just a normal day working in retail hell. My break's almost over and I gotta pee," Denise said, walking away.

Officer Wilson cracked her knuckles anxiously. Okay, so that had backfired. She would just have to find another way to figure out who had purchased the bullets. If only she could get access to the video surveillance.

"Can I see the video surveillance from that day?" She asked the customer service representative at the desk.

"Uh. I guess. But I don't think we have cameras near the checkout lanes, just at the front of the store and near the valuable or dangerous products."

"I would like to see it anyways. If I can identify someone I recognize entering the store or leaving the store with the bullets, it would help me solve the case or at least have tangible evidence that a suspect was here."

"Okay. Yeah. Just go through that door. All the camera footage is back there," the employee said, pointing.

"Thanks." Officer Wilson walked through the door and entered the surveillance room, which was full of large screens showing live footage from various vantage points near the entrance to the store, the outside of the building, and the valuable products. No one was in the small surveillance room, so she would have to find the footage by herself. She looked through the saved recordings until she found November 7th. She pressed play when the clock on the footage said 2:15 pm just to be safe and began watching the footage. She couldn't spot any of the suspects entering the store, so she continued watching until after the time stamp showed 2:30 pm to see if anyone exited with a case of bullets. A figure walked out of the store quickly with their head down, a large, baggy, black hoodie covering their face and any identifying features.

"Well, shit," she said, frustrated.

She asked the employee for permission to take the recording back to the NYPD as evidence, but by the time she was back at the

19th Precinct it was the end of the day. Officer Wilson left the police station in an agitated state and returned the next day to a disappointing discovery. There was a typed note on her desk, which said, *Officer Wilson, I know you found the surveillance of me at the store after I bought the bullets. I went back to get rid of the footage and discovered it wasn't there. I destroyed it, so don't try looking for it, or for me. You don't want to find me because if you do, it will be the last thing you do.*

CHAPTER 20:
Clara

Clara couldn't leave her apartment without being bombarded by reporters and their dozens of accusatory questions, as if she was the one responsible for Jackson's death. She hardly wanted to leave their apartment at all. *Their apartment.* In her mind, it still belonged to Jackson as much as it did to her. She supposed she should find a new place, but once she moved out it would seem as if she was shutting the door on a chapter of her life that would never exist. That chapter had been ripped out of the book and the rest of the pages were blank, waiting for her to make her next move, waiting for her to screw up.

As she fought her way through the crowd of reporters once again, one of them shoved a microphone in her face. "Did you have any involvement in the death of Jackson Birkman? Why did you do it? Were you after his money?"

So far, Clara had avoided answering any questions. Officer

Wilson had told her it was best to refrain from acknowledging the reporters because anything she said could become twisted if they decided it was a good story. Clara was done remaining quiet. She had enough of their prying.

She grabbed the microphone and all the reporters fell silent. "I loved Jackson. I still love him. Are you so insensitive that you can't see I'm mourning his loss? It just happened and it was unexpected. I had no warning or time to prepare myself. We were engaged; we were planning our future, which has been ripped out from under me, leaving me questioning everything." She paused to collect herself. She didn't want to cry in front of these nosey people. "I did not kill Jackson Birkman, but NYC has a great police force that is working hard to ensure the murderer is captured. I have faith that they will succeed. Now please leave me alone and let me mourn in peace."

The reporters slowly dispersed, most of them disappointed in the way she had finally broken her silence about Jackson's death. Clara handed the microphone back to the woman she had taken it from. The reporter made eye contact with her and smiled sympathetically, hitching her bag up higher on her shoulder and leaving Clara alone once again.

Clara was finally going back to work after taking several weeks off to recover and try her best to begin the healing process. She was still grieving immensely and felt as if that was taking everything out of her, so she didn't know how productive she would be once she was back in the office. Her boss had been understanding enough about the whole situation, but she dreaded returning to her job because she anticipated what was going to happen. Carl would try to comfort her with words of condolence and sympathy, and he would probably mean every word he said. But that wouldn't be the worst part. She knew it was going to be incredibly difficult to continue working without Jackson's encouragement and approval of her career choice. She had depended on him so much for the last six years; he had been a constant part of her life. There were days when she hated her job and could barely stand to get out of bed, but Jackson had always helped her push past that and continue working. It wasn't her dream job, not by a long shot, but the pay was decent enough and at least she had benefits. She knew she wouldn't be able to afford Jackson's apartment without his income though. She had already broken the lease at her old apartment, so she was going to have to figure something else out. Clara knew she might be able to play the sympathy card enough with Carl to convince him to give her a bonus or a raise. Then, she could at least have a few more months in the apartment until she figured out what to do next. Maybe she wouldn't even stay in New York. It had been Jackson's idea to move there to get a jumpstart on his acting career. Once he had landed the role of David on *Dispatching David*, it made sense for them to continue living in New York. But now, she supposed she had the freedom to move anywhere she wanted. With Jackson gone, his presence haunted her everywhere in the city she had never wanted to live in. As she traipsed through the once comfortingly familiar streets, she saw his ghost at their favorite Chinese restaurant, the theatre they frequented, the park where he had taken her for a picnic when they first moved to New York, and the coffee shop by their apartment where they had countless dates:

talking and laughing over their specialty coffees and freshly baked chocolate chip muffins.

Once Clara arrived at work, her co-workers paraded around her desk, each offering their sympathies, most of them not seeming sincere in the slightest. It was funny because she had never thought of her co-workers as uncaring or inconsiderate, but now it was as if she was seeing everyone for the first time. Blaine, one of her closest work friends, approached her desk last. He smiled at her and leaned against her desk.

"How are you?" He asked, touching her hand lightly.

Clara laughed, knowing this was the one person she could answer truthfully. "Awful." She carefully removed her hand from under his.

He glanced at her in appraisal, determining the best way to approach the topic. "I can't even imagine what you must be going through. It's one of those things you never expect to happen to you and then if you're unfortunate enough to have to go through it, you keep telling yourself over and over that it's all a nightmare, that soon you'll wake up and it will all be over."

"Exactly. God, I'm so glad someone understands. Everyone expects me to pick up with my normal life and go about working and living as if nothing is different, as if I didn't just go through the worst trauma of my life."

Blaine nodded. "I know how you feel. I lost my parents when I was young and it took me years to recover and finally forgive myself."

"What happened?" Clara asked, eager to change the subject from her own misfortune and surprised that Blaine had never revealed this information to her after their several years of friendship.

"They went on a cruise to the Bahamas for their anniversary when I was 7. The cruise ship struck a giant rock underwater and the ship began to submerge. Most of the passengers on the ship were able to escape on the lifeboats, but 100 people died during the accident. My parents didn't make it. They both drowned, presumably because there weren't enough lifeboats to save everyone. I was staying with my aunt during their trip, so she took me in and decided to adopt me after my parents died. I always felt guilty that she was forced to raise me, so I moved out as soon as I turned 18. I'm grateful she was kind enough to take care of me all those years and she did her best, but I know she didn't want to spend her life that way. She never wanted kids. She's a wonderful person, just not very motherly." Blaine sighed and shook his head as if to erase the pain. "Anyways, I know what it's like to miss someone you love and I also know how hard it is to adjust to living a normal life again. If you ever need to talk or get drunk on cheap wine and watch bad movies, I'm your guy."

"I'm so sorry about your parents, Blaine. That must have been hard for your aunt to suddenly have a child to take care of. And thanks. I might have to take you up on that sometime."

As close as she felt to Blaine, she realized they had never hung out outside of work. Probably because Jackson would have read too much into it and assumed something was going on between them.

Blaine stood up straighter and smiled softly, his dimples showing on either side of his mouth. "Well, take it easy today. It's only your first day back; it will take time to get into the swing of things again."

"Yeah. I don't know how much I will be able to get done, but I'll try my best." Clara smiled weakly in return and stared blankly at her computer screen. "I might call you over for help later. I feel like I can't concentrate on anything."

"Hey, don't worry about it," he said. "I'll stick around if you want. I could pull up a chair and help you finish the rest of your current project."

"Are you sure?" She asked apprehensively. "Don't you have your own stuff to do? I wouldn't want you to get behind..."

"Actually, I didn't want to tell you this, but since you've been gone, we have gotten extremely behind on your projects. We didn't want to hire someone to replace you and weren't sure when you would be coming back. I would rather help you catch up than miss more of our deadlines this month."

"Ugh. I'm sorry," she responded, groaning in frustration.

"It's not the end of the world. We still have time." He grabbed a chair from a nearby table and set it next to her desk. "I'll make a coffee run. I think we will need it. What do you want, a cappuccino?"

She nodded in appreciation. "That would be great. Thanks, Blaine."

"No problem. I'll be back soon. Is the coffee shop over on 72nd Street alright with you? I went there last week and fell in love. They have these amazing chocolate chip muffins..."

Clara winced. That was the coffee shop she and Jackson had frequented.

Blaine guessed the cause of her reaction. "You went there with Jackson?"

"Almost every week."

"I can go somewhere else if you want. There are a ton of coffee shops nearby."

"No. It's okay. I can't avoid everything that reminds me of him. Besides, their muffins are great."

"Okay then. Be back soon."

Blaine left and Clara continued staring at her computer screen, thankful she would have his steady presence to keep her on track for the remainder of the day. She scrolled through the pages of the article on her computer mindlessly, none of the words sinking in. She knew she had to at least finish editing this article today, if not several more, but that felt like an impossible task now. Blaine returned in what seemed like much too fast an amount of time and he gently reprimanded her for not getting anything done in his absence.

"I understand you're having trouble concentrating, but do you think you're ready to be back here yet? Maybe you should take the day off and go home. If you need more time off, no one is going to blame you."

Clara's face fell. She didn't want to disappoint anyone, especially someone who was being so kind about the loss of Jackson. "No. I want to work. I can do it." She took the cappuccino and muffin from the bag he was carrying and turned back to her computer screen. Enough caffeine could make anyone feel like they could conquer the world.

The day dragged on for Clara, however, despite the

encouragement and exorbitant amount of help from Blaine. He was trying his best to motivate her to finish and help her with the editing process as much as he could without explicitly doing the work for her, but despite his best efforts she didn't feel like she cared about her job anymore. Why did it matter if she finished editing this article and the half dozen other unfinished ones waiting for her? What was the point of any of it really? When she died, what would people remember about her? She would have nothing left, besides a few people who would mourn her. At least Jackson made an impact on the world. He changed lives. Millions of people knew his name and had been devastated after his accident, but what would happen if a horrific event caused her untimely death? Her parents would be the only ones who would miss her. And maybe Edgar and Blaine. No one else cared about her. The headlines would read "Jackson Birkman's Fiancée is Dead." That's all she would amount to, someone who was once engaged to a celebrity. It was a depressing thought.

At the end of the day, Blaine pulled her aside when she was getting ready to leave. He had stayed with her for a few hours, but then had to run off to take care of an issue with a client and was gone for the rest of the workday.

"I'm proud of you for making it through the day. I know you're still a tad behind, but I believe you can finish your current editorial projects on time and do a great job."

Clara sighed in relief and almost cried at his kind words. "That means so much. I'll try my best, I promise. I'm probably going to go home and pass out. I'm exhausted."

"Get some rest, Clara. I'll see you tomorrow."

She surprised him by throwing her arms around him in a hug. "Bye, Blaine," she said, letting go and swinging her purse over her shoulder as she left.

Blaine stared after her, watching her leave, knowing it was wrong of him to want her so badly, but at the same time not wanting to let go of the happiness he felt in her presence. And wasn't that the worst part about love? Not being able to choose who to love? Simply caring about someone because they made you want to be a better person, because they were worth it. Because your life was empty and meaningless without them in it. Because nothing seemed to faze you when they were around. Because love was the greatest feeling in the world and the worst and everything in between all at the same time.

He packed up his things and soon left the office as well. He went back to his apartment and made a frozen, microwaveable dinner as he did every night. He knew he couldn't let his feelings for Clara get in the way of their friendship. He had never outright told her, but he was sure that she knew. He suspected she might not get over Jackson and he foresaw that he would be the one to continuously pick up the pieces. But was that really what he wanted? Maybe if things had been different, if he had told her when Jackson was still alive, or if she had never been with Jackson…maybe then they would be together. It was too late to wonder about all the what if's or what could have been. All he had was now and that would have to be enough.

Meanwhile, Clara was back at her apartment as well. She had fed Henry and picked up an extra-large pepperoni pizza on her way home. She didn't care about being healthy for the time being.

Screw it. She could eat three pieces of pepperoni pizza and not feel guilty about the calories. She sat on her couch, curled up in a fuzzy blanket, watching HGTV. It kept her mind off things enough to finally stop thinking and drift off to sleep. Henry joined her, kneading his paws into her until she woke up and petted him. They fell asleep together, each of them enjoying the comfort and love of another living thing, each content in their own way.

When she woke up the next morning, she was immediately in a panic. She hadn't set an alarm or laid out work clothes for the day or prepared for the morning in any way as she usually did. Clara threw on dress pants and a collared shirt that wasn't noticeably wrinkled, deciding she didn't have enough time to shower. She had planned to pick up a coffee for Blaine to thank him for yesterday, but she didn't have time now. She barely had time to tame her extremely frizzy hair and apply mascara before rushing towards the office. She would have to fight off her hunger until lunch because she didn't have time to cook breakfast. Anyways, she had neglected to go grocery shopping for weeks, so she didn't even have the option of grabbing yogurt or a granola bar on her way out the door.

Clara arrived at the office on time and wildly threw down her purse and coat when she sat at her desk. Today was already off to a bad start and she hadn't even begun working yet. It was going to be another long, grueling day. She didn't want to hate her job, but she had to muster all her strength to drag herself to work and force herself to be productive, when she would much rather quit or fling herself off the top story of the office building. Not seriously. But she considered it, at least for a few seconds, enough to pause and contemplate the effects of her suicide. It would be so easy to give in, but it wasn't worth it. She didn't want to die, she realized. She wanted to live. As much as she loved Jackson and missed him and didn't want to find out how her life would turn out without him, she wanted to live even more.

The Long Shadow on the Stage

CHAPTER 21:
Clara

Clara came home from work still laughing from a ridiculous joke Blaine had told her earlier. He was trying everything he could to make her smile and she found that being around him did make things a bit easier to handle. As Clara approached the door of her apartment, she saw Henry's tiny body crudely nailed to the door; dried blood had dripped grotesquely down the door. Henry's eyes were wide open and his once sleek, soft gray fur was matted and covered in blood. It looked as if his throat had been slit. What kind of monster would kill her precious kitten? He was only a few months old and she hadn't even had him very long yet. She couldn't bear the thought of Henry meowing and whimpering as some sick person had harmed him. He was just an innocent animal. She hated herself for not being there to protect him. She cowered to the ground, sobbing hugely, wracking her body with the effort her cries expelled. As she fell, she fainted.

When she awoke an hour later, she shakily pulled herself to her feet and gathered herself to look at her poor kitten. She supposed she would have to call Officer Wilson and tell her what had happened. She turned to look at the door and didn't immediately register what she saw. None of the horror she had witnessed earlier was visible. Henry's body was gone, without a trace of the nails or any blood. She turned wildly, her eyes straining down the hallway. She caught a glimpse of a figure running towards the stairs and sprinted after them. She still felt slightly dizzy, but she was determined to find out who had killed her cat. She caught up to the figure, who had a huge parka covering them, so their face wasn't visible. Clara tackled the figure, wanting answers.

"What did you do to my cat, you monster?" She shrieked.

The hooded figure squeaked. It was Mrs. Dell, her neighbor from down the hall. She was wearing a parka because of the cold weather, so her face was protected from the cold but also obscured from Clara's eyes until now. "Get off of me!"

Clara jumped up, reaching out her hand to help Mrs. Dell to her feet. "I'm so sorry!" She apologized. "My cat was killed and nailed to my apartment door. When I saw you running down the hallway, I thought you were the one who did it. I'm so sorry, Mrs. Dell."

"Crazy girl. There's nothing on your door," Mrs. Dell said, after looking towards her apartment, then ignoring Clara's hand and slowly getting back on her feet. She brushed off her coat and stared coldly at Clara. "You can't just go around knocking over your elders. Young people have no respect anymore. It's because you're all raised without punishment or consequences for your actions."

Mrs. Dell began walking towards the stairs again, muttering to herself. "Stupid girl."

"Wait, Mrs. Dell! You didn't happen to see someone near my apartment earlier, did you?" Clara questioned desperately.

"Why would I help you after you nearly killed me?"

"Please. My cat is dead. I just need to know if you saw anyone near my apartment."

"Well, as a matter of fact, I did. There was a young man, about your age, who went by earlier. He said hello to me. He helped me carry my groceries inside. He was very charming."

"A young man? What did he look like?" Clara asked, panicking. Who had gotten into her apartment? Was it the same person who had set up Jackson's death?

Mrs. Dell thought for a minute. "Hmm. He had long hair." She shrugged her shoulders and continued walking.

"Is that all you remember?" Clara implored.

"Ah, yes. He had these brown eyes that were quite haunting. Like he had been through a lot in his life. That's all I remember and I have a doctor's appointment that I don't care to be late to. My husband's waiting for me in the car," she said, pushing open the door to the stairwell and leaving Clara alone in the hallway.

Clara stood immobile for a moment, contemplating what Mrs. Dell had told her. Someone with long hair and haunting brown eyes. *Edgar?* She wondered fleetingly, then quickly shook away the absurd thought. Edgar would never do something like that. He was Jackson's best friend. She pulled out her cell phone and dialed the number of the police station.

"Hi, this is Clara. Can I speak to Officer Wilson? It's important."

Officer Wilson showed up quickly, considering she had been across town when Clara called. She followed Clara over to her apartment and pulled out her gun.

"It's just a precaution," she explained, noticing the alarmed look on Clara's face. "I'll enter the apartment first and let you know when it's safe. I want to make sure whoever killed your cat isn't waiting in your apartment."

Clara nodded, too scared to speak. She was ripping her nails to shreds, as she always did when she was nervous or anxious. She felt comforted that Officer Wilson had responded so quickly and that she was willing to scout out her apartment.

"It's safe, Clara," Officer Wilson called out a few minutes later from inside of the apartment.

Clara slowly entered the apartment, looking around, searching for anything out of the ordinary.

"Everything looks fine. It could have just been a break-in."

Clara bit her lip. "A break-in where they murdered my cat?"

"I want to believe this is unrelated to Jackson's case, but it's too soon to know for sure," Officer Wilson said. "What would they have done with your cat though? You said your cat was nailed to your front door?"

"He was, but I fainted and when I woke up Henry was gone. Why would they take his body? And how did they know I saw it? Do you think they were watching me from somewhere nearby?" Clara asked, tears welling up in her eyes. She didn't think she could handle another traumatic experience. She had gone through far too much already. Henry was supposed to be her comfort, her companion so she wasn't lonely and depressed. She wasn't equipped to deal with more tragedy.

"We are clearly dealing with a sick person. I'll write up a report when I get back to the station."

"That's it?"

"There's not much else I can do, I'm afraid. I'm sorry about your cat." Officer Wilson inspected the outside of the door before she left. She hesitated. "Are you sure you saw your cat nailed to the door? You described a pretty graphic scene and there is no evidence to show that anything happened."

"I swear that's what I saw! Don't you believe me?"

"I do, it's just…" She looked at the lock of the door and then looked back at Clara. "There's no sign of forced entry into your apartment. Did anyone else have a key, other than you and Jackson? What happened to his key when he died?"

"No one else has a key. And I don't know. It was probably in his jeans pocket when he died. That's where he always kept it. I never thought about it."

"Could someone have gotten his key somehow?"

"I don't think so. They would have had to be around him before he died. Unless it was someone who was on the set with him that day."

Clara looked at Officer Wilson with such a pitiful look that Officer Wilson felt terribly bad for her. She had been through so much the past few weeks.

"Is that what you think, Officer?" Clara asked. "It was

someone he worked with on the show?"

Officer Wilson didn't respond for a minute, debating how best to continue but wanting to be honest with Clara. "I believe so."

CHAPTER 22

I touched the key to the apartment, which was safely tucked away in the pocket of my jeans. 13A was emblazoned on the apartment door. As I was walking down the hallway, I spotted an elderly woman struggling to carry her groceries. She was fumbling for her keys.

"Do you need help?" I asked.

"Oh, yes, that would be lovely! Thank you."

I grabbed a few of the bags from her arms so she could unlock the door and helped her carry the groceries inside her apartment. I set the bags down on her kitchen counter and turned to leave.

"Most young people don't want to go out of their way to help strangers," the old woman said. "I appreciate your kindness."

"It was no problem at all," I told her, smiling. "Have a good day."

I left her apartment and headed back towards 13A down the hallway. As I unlocked the door, a tiny gray kitten immediately greeted me, purring against my legs. "Hey there, little guy," I said softly, picking him up to pet him and closing the door. I carried him into the kitchen and opened a can of cat food, which I plopped into his food dish. He immediately began eating and several minutes later, the food dish was empty.

"Come here," I said, gently grabbing him and pulling a bottle of *Pet Wellbeing Stress Gold* out of my pocket. I pried open his mouth and placed a few drops on his tongue, but more of the liquid sedative than I intended spilled out of the bottle and into his mouth. The tiny gray kitten choked and struggled, scratching my arms with his claws, trying to free himself.

Several minutes later, the kitten was sedated. I threw down several newspapers on the kitchen floor and placed him on top of them. The kitten's small chest was rising slightly as he breathed, sleeping peacefully. I found a large knife in the kitchen and held it to the kitten's throat. "Sweet dreams," I said, suddenly slicing the knife across his throat before I could lose my nerve.

CHAPTER 23:
Edgar

Edgar and Jackson were meeting at their usual coffeeshop. It was the same coffeeshop Jackson and Clara frequently visited together. Edgar acted like it didn't bother him, but he wished they had a place that was just theirs. Almost every aspect of their relationship had been tainted by Clara's presence. Edgar was startled from his thoughts as Jackson sat at the chair across from him at the small bistro table they usually chose.

"Hey, Edgar," Jackson greeted him, smiling.

"How's it going? You look the happiest you have been in a while," Edgar said cautiously.

Jackson's smile spread across his entire face. "Wouldn't you like to know?" He asked coyly.

Edgar laughed. "Well, what is it? What happened?" He asked, playing into Jackson's game. Jackson never outright told him any news. Edgar always had to beg him for information before he finally caved.

"I'm going to order a coffee. You want one?" Jackson asked, abruptly changing the subject.

"Sure, thanks. Just make sure-"

"Yeah, I know. Cream and sugar. You should just drink it black like me. It's cheaper and healthier."

"It's too bitter without cream and sugar," Edgar said, wrinkling his nose. "I don't know how you drink it like that."

Jackson rolled his eyes and went to the counter to purchase their coffees.

When he came back several minutes later, Edgar leaned forward eagerly, anticipating the news Jackson had that was making him so happy. "So, are you going to tell me or what? Why are you so giddy?"

"Let's just say there's a new cast member on *Dispatching David* and she-"

Edgar groaned and took a sip of his overly sweet coffee. "Jackson, not again. How could you do that to Clara?"

"All I said was there is a new cast member. I didn't do anything wrong," Jackson said in protest.

"I know where you were going with that line of thought. I saw the new cast member. Sandra, isn't it? She isn't your usual type."

"I know. Believe me, it surprised me too, but man, she's hot."

"Stay away from her, Jackson. Don't screw up your relationship with Clara over some random girl."

"Since when do you care so much about Clara and I?" Jackson asked, raising an eyebrow.

"I may not have been the biggest fan of Clara in the beginning, but I have grown to appreciate the impact she has on you. I think she's good for you. You need someone like her in your life."

Jackson snorted and almost spit out his coffee. "Nah. I don't need Clara's "positive influence" when I already have you."

"As much as I appreciate the sentiment, I don't think getting involved with another woman while you're in a relationship is a good idea."

"Edgar, loosen up a bit. It's not like I'm married. Besides, this is purely hypothetical. I've barely spoken to Sandra."

"Then I suggest you stop while you're ahead."

Jackson sighed dramatically and sipped his steaming black coffee. "We'll see. Anyways, I asked you to meet me here for a different reason."

Edgar stayed silent, waiting for Jackson to tell him whatever it was he wanted this time. He was almost certain Jackson was going to ask him for more money.

"Well, uh," Jackson said, awkwardly, scratching at the dark stubble on his chin. "I know I promised last time would be the last time, but things keep coming up which is making it harder to pay you back. Jessica asked me for a few thousand dollars so she would have enough to buy a new car. Her car unexpectedly died last week. She never asks me for anything, so it was the least I could do."

"Jackson, that is exactly what you should not be doing right now! That's how you got into this situation! Did you at least tell Jessica you were going to charge interest on the money she borrowed?"

"I didn't really tell her it was a loan," Jackson said sheepishly.

"What did you say? You just gave her the money?"

"That's what you did for me…"

Edgar paused. "Yeah, but that's different. We're best friends and you had no one else to turn to."

"It's not that different. She's my sister. She would never ask my parents for help, so I was the only person she could ask for the money. Besides, if I told her I didn't have the money, that would be a red flag. She would have to ask my parents for help and I don't want to find out how they would react if they found out how much debt I'm in."

"Jackson, I did you a favor and I don't regret loaning you the money, but do you intend on ever paying me back?"

Jackson sipped his coffee in silence for a minute. "I fully intend on paying you back, Edgar; I just need more time. I know I said before that it was the last time, but I swear, this will be the last time for real."

Edgar fidgeted and adjusted his glasses, then stared into his coffee cup at the light brown coffee which was so much lighter than the black of Jackson's coffee. He pulled his wallet out of his jacket pocket and pried a check out of the wallet. "How much?"

"Oh, Edgar, you're the greatest, dude!" Jackson immediately responded. "I think five thousand will cover it. And really, I *promise* this is it. No more loans."

CHAPTER 24:
Edgar

Edgar saw his reflection in the TV screen and noticed how haunted he looked. His appearance was haggard, with days of stubble on his face, his hair longer and scragglier than ever, dark circles accentuated underneath his eyes. He was hanging out with Clara in her apartment. They were eating Mexican food, which Jackson hated but they both loved. They sat on the couch Clara despised in the sitting room, watching HGTV as they ate dinner.

"You don't mind watching this?" Clara asked, raising an eyebrow.

"Honestly, I watch it all the time when I'm alone," Edgar admitted. "The Property Brothers are my favorite."

"Mine too. They make it more entertaining than most of the other home decorating shows. Plus, I like their decorating style the best."

"Mhm," Edgar responded over a mouthful of beef enchilada.

"God, Jackson would kill us if he knew we were eating on his couch."

Edgar stared at her, wondering if she realized what she had just said. "Yeah."

"Sometimes I pretend," she said, setting her plate down on the coffee table. "That he's not dead. I imagine he's away on a vacation, a business trip, or visiting his family in Minnesota. But he'll be back soon and I'll see him again. He's not really gone. Just for a little while. It's only temporary."

Edgar patted her on the shoulder. "It's easier to cope if you think that way," he agreed.

"But of course, I know he's dead. If I ever find out who killed him…"

"What would you do?"

"Don't you want revenge? Do you ever think about it, Edgar? You loved him too. I know you did." She noticed the astonished look on his face. "Not in the same way, of course," she said quickly. "But still."

"I did love him," Edgar said, feeling free for a moment. "I loved him so much."

"Me too."

"And you're right. Not in the same way you loved him. I loved him even more. I loved him despite all his imperfections and annoying habits. I helped him with his financial problems and never questioned his choices. I was the one who bailed him out time after time. He came to me for everything. I lived with him for much longer than you, I knew him for years, and most of our lives were spent together. We were two halves of one perfect whole. No,

I didn't love him the same as you at all."

"What do you…?"

"Oh, Clara. How simple it must be for you to mourn his death freely and without shame. It's not that easy for me. It's much more complicated. I'm tied up in guilt because it's my fault. I wish I hadn't been the one to pull the trigger. But how could I have known? How could I have stopped it?"

"I- I don't know," she stuttered, becoming increasingly confused. "It wasn't your fault. Some sick person is the one who switched the guns and the police are going to figure out who did it. The police will take care of everything. I know Officer Wilson and she promised she would solve the case," Clara said, sounding reminiscent of a stubborn child refusing to believe anything other than what she wanted to be the truth.

"Do you really believe that? The police in this city are a bunch of morons. They're too preoccupied with the fact that it's a celebrity's death. They don't care about finding out who set up the murder. They want the case wrapped up as quickly as possible and you can bet they're going to do a sloppy job and miss something."

"Edgar, stop it. That's not true. Don't you believe in the greater good? Don't you think the murderer will be convicted and sent to prison? Don't you believe there's hope to cling onto and the promise of happiness and better days in the future once all of this is over?"

"I don't believe that anymore. I can't."

"What has made you give up? I never thought of you as a pessimistic person before…"

"It's just…something that happens when you start seeing the

world the way it really is. Nothing in this world is truly good because every bright and shining thing has a side that is its opposite: ugly and dark."

CHAPTER 25:
Edgar

Edgar lived a lonely life. Or at least it appeared that way to others. His parents didn't agree with his life choices and he hadn't talked to them in over two years. He was an only child. There weren't many people he cared about, besides Jackson. Now that Jackson was gone, he retreated to his hermit lifestyle. It was comfortable for him. Edgar didn't mind being alone in the slightest. He liked being able to have his own schedule and not worry about bothering anyone else. Besides, after losing Jackson, he didn't want to get close to anyone. He needed time to drown in his thoughts, to feel the pain of loss until it filled up his mind completely, overflowing into every sentence he spoke, thought, or dreamt. Much of his time was spent reading anything he could get his hands on. The characters in his novels were the only people he needed. He drew comfort from the words of others, knowing that they had taken a great amount of care, not to mention time, to create a world that others wanted to get lost in and characters that were relatable to readers. He didn't need much to be happy, but he was beginning to grow weary of searching for a new way to earn a living.

Edgar didn't know what to do with himself now that *Dispatching David* was ending this week. He felt the same panic Jackson had felt months ago. He hadn't planned for what would happen next. He began auditioning for anything he thought he would enjoy, which included several TV shows, and even a low-budget indie film that seemed interesting. His resume was far from impressive when compared with the thousands of other actors and actresses in NYC, but he kept trying with the hope for something great. The problem was he wouldn't settle for anything short of extraordinary. He turned down several offers for commercials and a role on a Lifetime movie. He didn't want to become a sellout. He and Jackson had always mocked those actors who were in one TV show, then vanished off the face of the Earth, wondering what could happen to make them stop acting, but now he was beginning to understand. Landing acting roles was not going to be as easy as it had been so far for him. He had been lucky that Jackson had gotten him the role on *Dispatching David*. As much as it pained him to admit, he knew he couldn't have done it without him. In the meantime, though, he had money saved. He would be fine for a while.

His cell phone rang unexpectedly as he was turning the pages of a worn copy of "Great Expectations," one of his favorite novels. He answered the phone and carefully shut his novel, marking his place with a bookmark.

"Hello?"

"Hello, is this Edgar Peterson?"

"Yes, it is," he said hesitantly.

"This is Maura, the director of *The Quest*. I loved your audition and was wondering if you were still interested in the role."

Edgar gasped in excitement and nearly dropped his cell phone. "Yes, I'm definitely interested!" He replied eagerly.

"Great. Callbacks are tomorrow at 7 pm. We have the lead actress cast already and we want to make sure the lead actor has good chemistry with her. Show up a half hour early and sign in at the front desk."

"That sounds great. Thank you so much!"

Edgar hung up and stared at his cell phone in awe. *The Quest* was the indie film he had been dying to be in. It would be amazing if he had a chance to be in a movie, even if it was one with a small budget and a cast of actors and actresses who weren't well-known. He wouldn't be paid a ton of money, but the exposure would be decent, and the script looked entertaining, to say the least. He imagined going to the movie theater in a year or two when the movie was released. There would be a lit-up poster with his face and name plastered across it. He would see himself on the big screen and it would be everything he had ever dreamed of.

Edgar didn't think he was getting ahead of himself because he didn't see how anyone else could possibly stand a chance at getting the role. At the auditions, there had been dozens of dull males who were severely lacking both talent and looks. He was a trained actor; he had been on an award-winning TV show for God's sakes. He deserved it and there wasn't anything he wouldn't do to make sure he got the lead role. He began preparing for the callback, practicing monologues he had used for auditions recently, and carefully choosing an outfit for the occasion. He wanted to look the part, so Maura knew without a doubt there was no one better suited for the role than Edgar.

The next night he arrived at the studio nearly an hour early and excitedly paced across the floor until the other actors started showing up. He was the first one to sign in and he sized up the others as he waited to be called onto the stage. They were worthless, every single one of them. They stood there in their cheaply made dress clothes, obviously knock-off designers', and anxiously looked around the room, muttering to themselves and each other about how terrified/nervous/overwhelmed they were about callbacks. Edgar just paced and smiled to himself, his confidence growing by the minute.

One of the younger actors approached him. "Aren't you Edgar Peterson?" He asked in awe.

"Yes, I am," Edgar said, smiling and shaking the man's hand.

"Did you get a callback for Lucas also?" The young man asked, wringing his hands.

"Yes," He said in a slightly colder tone.

"I'm sure you'll get it," the young man said. "I don't know why they wouldn't just give it to you. Most of the guys here are worthless," he continued.

"Everyone that is here tonight deserves a callback," Edgar said. "If the director didn't think so, then we wouldn't be here."

"You're right, I guess. God, I'm so nervous. I've never had an audition for a role like this before. I did theatre in high school and college. I was Titus in *Titus Andronicus* my senior year. That role was one of the most difficult I've ever done. But I've done all small-scale plays, never more than a few hundred people in the audience, and I've never been paid for acting. I just thought I would audition and see what happened," he rambled. "Hey, do you have any advice? You're a great actor and you were on a TV show, so you must know exactly how these things go, right?"

"I do have a bit of experience," Edgar responded with a wry smile. "Make sure you look confident. Say your lines clearly and make sure to enunciate. And when the scene is over, thank the director and anyone else in the room for their time."

"Okay. Yeah. I hope it's my turn soon. I don't know how much longer I can wait."

"What's your name?" Edgar asked.

"Carter."

"Carter, the best advice I can give you is to calm down and stop worrying about the role so much. If you're too nervous, it will spill over into your role and make your acting appear sloppy. Honestly, you're going to be rejected many times and you won't get some of your dream roles, even when you think you deserve them. It's going to be hard, but if this is the career you've chosen, it's one that is meaningful and rewarding."

"Thanks, Edgar." Carter paused, as if he was about to say something else, but changed his mind.

Edgar noticed. "What?"

"I'm sorry about Jackson," he said.

Edgar stiffened. "Thanks." He turned away from Carter and pretended to be busy looking at something on his cellphone.

Carter chose to ignore that and continued talking, "That's so crazy someone switched the guns and that you were the one who shot him. Weren't you guys friends in real life?"

Edgar put his cell phone back in his pocket and turned to face Carter again. "Yeah, it is "crazy." It was also horrific and traumatizing because Jackson was my best friend. But that's really none of your business, so shut the hell up and leave me alone, kid."

"Geez, okay," Carter said, backing away. "I was just asking. You didn't have to be such a dick about it."

Edgar strode forward, intending to punch Carter with all the force he could muster. Just then, Maura called out, "Edgar? Edgar Peterson?"

Edgar turned towards her and smiled hugely, shaking away his anger at Carter and preparing himself for his callback. "I'm Edgar."

"Come on in," Maura said in a welcoming tone. "Cassandra will be reading the scene with you. She will be playing the role of Nikki. You may begin as soon as you're ready."

CHAPTER 26:
Clara

Clara was sitting on the ugly leather couch that Jackson had refused to get rid of, even when she had begged him. She still hated it. Almost everything in the apartment was Jackson's. He had chosen all the furniture, everything in the kitchen except her coffeemaker, and the hundreds of DVDs and video games he had accumulated over the years were organized on floor-to-ceiling shelves in the family room in a massive entertainment center. The bedroom was the only room that felt remotely like hers and that was only because Jackson's parents had taken as many of Jackson's belongings as they could when they flew back to Minnesota. She had just gotten home from meeting Blaine for coffee and was feeling guilty. Realistically, she knew she couldn't mourn Jackson's death forever. Of course, she knew a part of her would always miss him, but wouldn't he have wanted her to move on, to find someone else to fall in love with and make her happy?

That didn't mean she had stopped loving Jackson or that she was in love with Blaine, but being around Blaine was making it easier for her to feel like things would be okay.

Edgar was coming over soon, so she was trying her best to push away her downtrodden thoughts. Although, she knew that out of everyone, Edgar would be the most likely to understand how she was feeling.

There was a knock on the door and she jumped up to answer it. Edgar stood there, holding a gigantic bottle of white wine.

Clara smirked. "Geez, Edgar, planning on doing some drinking tonight?"

Edgar smiled. "Maybe a bit."

"I was thinking we could go out for dinner though. I've been living off takeout the past few weeks, but I don't feel like cooking."

"Sounds good. We can grab dinner somewhere and come back here afterwards for drinks. What did you have in mind?"

Clara hesitated. "Romano's? It's that Italian place down the street. Jackson took me there after he proposed and I haven't been back there since then. All their food is amazing. The owner and his wife moved here from Italy in the 60's so it's authentic Italian food."

"I've never gone there before, but sure. I'm down for whatever," Edgar said cheerily.

"You seem like you're in a good mood," Clara responded, putting on her black wool coat and grabbing her purse.

"Well, I can't be depressed forever," Edgar said, setting down the bottle of wine on the kitchen counter. "Besides, don't you think Jackson would want us to be happy?"

"I was actually contemplating the same thing just before you got here."

"Oh yeah?"

"Yeah. Just that Jackson would want me to be happy even if that means moving on."

"What do you mean by moving on?" Edgar paused in the kitchen, his hand tightening around the wine bottle.

Clara sighed as she pulled mittens on her fingers and adjusted her hat. "Edgar, I know it hasn't been very long, but I have been spending time with Blaine lately and-"

"Who's *Blaine*?"

"He's a friend of mine, someone I work with. He has been so great throughout this whole tragedy. He has been there for me through everything and has been so patient and understanding."

"What are you trying to say, Clara?"

Clara's eyes widened as she realized how Edgar must feel. "I'm sorry, Edgar. It's not that you haven't been helping me because you have been a huge help. It's nice talking to you and spending time with you reminiscing about Jackson. You were his best friend and you knew him better than anyone besides me, so it's comforting to have you around. But..." She hesitated, unsure of what else to say and unsure of how she felt towards Blaine as well. "To be honest, I'm not sure what exactly will happen with Blaine. For now, we're just friends and maybe that's all we ever will be. I'm not ready for a relationship yet. I know how all of this must sound..."

"How could you, Clara? It has only been a few months and you're already going on dates with one of your co-workers?

Besides, what do you even know about Blaine?"

"I understand you're upset, but I promise he's a wonderful person. I've known him for several years, ever since I started my job. He's my closest work friend and he's kind of had a crush on me for a while. Of course, nothing ever happened because I didn't think of him like that and I was with Jackson. But he's so smart and charming and he's cute, which doesn't hurt," she said with a smile.

"Are you sure?" Edgar asked, raising an eyebrow. "You never hung out with this Blaine guy while you were with Jackson?"

"No, Jackson met him at one of my company's summer cookouts when I first started working there. After he saw the way Blaine kept staring at me and how he acted around me, he didn't want me spending any time with him outside of work, so I never did."

"I don't think I believe you. I bet you were sneaking around spending time with Blaine and hiding it from Jackson."

"Edgar, I don't- Why would you think that? I would never do anything to hurt Jackson."

"I don't know, Clara, maybe because it has only been a few months since your fiancé died. His body is barely cold in the grave and you're hanging out with a potential suitor!"

"You were just saying… Don't you think Jackson would want me to be happy, even if it was with someone else?"

"Your happiness isn't worth that much in the grand scheme of things."

Clara's eyes began to brim with tears. "You don't think my happiness is worth it if I'm not with Jackson? Is that what you really think? Why have you been spending so much time with me if you think so little of me?"

Edgar pulled his hair hard, spastically tried to make himself stop, and pulled his hair again. "I only wanted to be around you because you know things about Jackson that I'll never know. Things I wanted to know but never could," he said softly.

"I think you should leave," Clara said, wiping her tear-streaked face and trying to compose herself.

Edgar frowned. "Look, I'm sorry... I shouldn't have said that your happiness doesn't matter. I took it too far. I know you are dealing with a lot right now after Jackson's death and then Henry's. I can see how it would help to have a nice distraction like an attractive man paying attention to you."

Clara paused from wiping her face with tissues. "What? How did you know about Henry? I never told anyone except Officer Wilson. I was going to tell you tonight, but- How could you have known? Did you talk to Officer Wilson after I saw her?"

"I just assumed something happened to him because he usually greets me immediately when I come over. And I didn't see him on the couch or lying in his bed in the living room. I assumed something was wrong. Was he sick? Or did he get out of the apartment somehow and get hit by a car?"

"I don't know how you knew about Henry, but your explanation doesn't cut it. I want you to leave. *Now,*" Clara said emphatically, folding her arms across her chest and trying to appear as tough as possible, even though she suddenly felt terrified of Edgar.

"Fine, fine. I'll go. All I wanted was to grab dinner with a friend and drink some wine, but apparently that was me asking for too much out of life," Edgar said, rolling his eyes.

"You clearly don't think of me as a friend after talking to me the way you just did. Goodbye, Edgar," Clara said, opening the front door of her apartment in a showy wave.

CHAPTER 27:
Edgar

Edgar knew what he had to do. Clara knew far too much. She had found out about Jackson's debt and how he had been helping him financially for over three years. She knew that he understood Jackson better than anyone and that he cared deeply for Jackson, perhaps in the same way that she cared for him. It was all too much to handle. He couldn't let her find out anything else. It had been fun being friends with her, really, he had enjoyed himself the past few months and almost wished they had become close sooner. Maybe then things could have ended differently. But it was too late for that.

The next day, he knocked on the door of Clara's apartment. She answered the door and smiled slightly as she saw the exquisite bouquet of flowers he was holding.

"How did you know I like hydrangeas?" She said, taking the flowers from him and beginning to search her apartment for a vase.

"I remembered Jackson mentioning it at some point," he said sheepishly.

"Well, that was nice of you to remember. Why did you stop by though? I'm still upset with you about yesterday. I appreciate the gesture, but I'm not just going to forget about the hurtful things you said to me. This doesn't make up for it."

"Look, I'm really sorry, Clara. I shouldn't have said that your happiness doesn't matter. Of course it does. I was lashing out at you because I felt betrayed that you're starting to date someone else and I thought Jackson would feel betrayed too. I was only trying to be a good friend to Jackson."

"Edgar, that does *not* excuse what you said! I know Jackson was your best friend and you guys knew each other almost your entire lives, but he's gone now. I'm learning how to move on and I think you should too."

"What if I don't want to move on?"

"I don't really think you have a choice unless you want to keep wallowing in self-pity and depression for the rest of your life. You should get out of your apartment more and hang out with other people besides me. Make some new friends. Try a new hobby. Get outside of your comfort zone."

"I don't think that will help."

"Well, at least try, Edgar." Clara glanced at the time on her phone. "I hate to rush you out, but I was about to go meet Blaine for dinner."

"Don't worry. This won't take long," Edgar said, shutting the door.

***

Edgar sauntered into the Glass Tower building, where the TV show was filmed. It was the last day of filming *Dispatching David*. In a way, he felt sad to be leaving the show. It was the first major acting role he ever had. It was his chance to prove himself as an actor and show the world that Jackson wasn't entirely responsible for getting him onto the show. He was an actor of his own volition and he deserved recognition for his talent. Once everyone arrived, Gus called the actors and production crew to circle around him.

"This is the last time we will all be in this building for the show. It's the last scene and it's the most important because the dedicated fans have been waiting five years to see what would happen to David at the end. They're all dying to know if he will get what he deserves or if he will get away with everything. Edgar, we're counting on you to make the ending go smoothly, so we can have a successful airing of the last episode. Once we finish filming, there will be a cast party at The Plaza. The episode will air in a few weeks at the usual time. Break legs, everyone!"

Edgar nervously broke from the circle of his colleagues and spoke up. "Thanks for this opportunity, Gus. And thank you, everyone, for all your support and encouragement the past few weeks, not just with the show, but with your sympathy over Jackson's untimely death. You have been a great help to my healing process because you all knew firsthand how talented, smart, and great Jackson was. So, thank you for your kind words and-"

Gus cut him off. "Does this look like a platform for airing your personal problems?"

"I just wanted everyone to know their kind words and

sympathy was appreciated..." Edgar said.

"Well, now they know. Get your ass on the set."

Edgar hesitated momentarily and Gus barked out, "NOW!"

Lights up. Camera rolling. Kevin entered the kitchen, setting the bag containing several Chinese take-out boxes on the white marble counter.

"Mary?" He called out. Usually when he arrived home from work, Mary was in the living room reading and enjoying a glass of wine. That was how she had been spending her evenings lately. "Mary, I brought Chinese food for dinner!"

Kevin kicked off his shoes and walked down the hallway into their bedroom. He heard what sounded like grunting and a moan, so he paused uncertainly by the closed bedroom door. Was Mary watching porn? He knocked on the door and heard Mary say, "Shit!"

"What the fuck?" Kevin screamed as he opened the door.

David jumped up from the bed, wrapping the blanket around his torso so his muscular chest was apparent. "Kevin, listen, just calm down. We can talk about it if you give me a chance to explain."

Mary jumped up from the bed, completely naked, frantically searching for her clothes.

"Explain what? How I just got home from a late night of working to find you fucking my wife?" Kevin said, spit flying from his mouth in anger.

"Calm down so we can talk this out, Kevin. Please," David said.

The show continued filming until the much-anticipated

gunshot scene. Everyone waited with bated breath to see what would happen the second time filming the scene. This time, there wasn't a startlingly loud gunshot, or a bullet flying through the air to force itself through flesh and exit through the back of a head, which had fallen to the ground with a sickening thud. Edgar lay on the ground for several seconds, while the actor who played Kevin stared at the gun, then the body in front of him. He looked at the camera, breaking the fourth wall and said, "Some things can be forgiven. Others…will haunt you forever. This can't be forgiven, but in time, maybe I can forget it all and move on. I don't know what the future will entail, but maybe things will get better. Maybe I will learn to love again or maybe more promising things are yet to come. All I know is that I'm hopeful for a better tomorrow."

Everyone clapped and cheered after the lights went down and the cameras stopped rolling.

"That's a wrap!" Gus yelled. "We're done!"

"How was it?" Edgar asked, rushing offstage to talk to Gus. He wanted to know how his acting was in his final scene for the show.

"Good enough to air," Gus said with a snort.

Edgar's face fell with disappointment. He thought he had been at his best; he felt as if he finally pulled himself away from reality and into the world in which David was immersed, but maybe he was wrong. "Did it look okay? I mean, I didn't screw anything up too badly, right?" He asked for reassurance.

The actor who played Kevin came over to him and clapped him on the shoulder. "Don't worry, Edgar. I think you were great. I really felt it in the scene. It felt real."

"It did for me too. And thanks. You were great too. I'm glad that since I had to have a replacement, it was you."

"That means a lot. Really though, don't worry about Gus." He said comfortingly.

"Okay, girls, you were fantastic. Feel better now?" Gus asked with a sneer. "The scene was fine; your acting was fine…"

"So, are we going to have a viewing party since it was the last episode?" Edgar asked.

"Nope. That's up to you to watch it on your own time. I have a new TV show that I'm supposed to start directing next week, so I don't have time to dwell on past jobs. I have too much going on right now," Gus said.

"You do? What's the show about?"

Gus smiled in what appeared to be a kind manner. "The show has already been cast. Sorry, princess."

"I wasn't trying to-"

"No, no. Of course, you weren't. Anyways, it was nice working with you. Good luck with your future acting career," Gus said, extending his hand to shake cordially.

Edgar shook his head and smiled disbelievingly. Leave it to Gus to part like this. "Thanks for the opportunity, Gus. It was a pleasure working with you," he replied.

Gus responded with the most authentic laugh Edgar had ever heard from him. "In all my years of being a director, I have never heard anyone say that I'm a pleasure to work with. I appreciate the sentiment, princess, but nice job trying to get on my good side. I know I can be a pain in the ass to work with, so you don't have to pretend like it was some great role that you thoroughly enjoyed and that we were pals. I know the truth and the truth sits better with me than some pretty little lies do."

The Long Shadow on the Stage

CHAPTER 28:
Officer Wilson

Officer Wilson knocked on the door of Clara's apartment for the second time; this time she called out, "Clara?" But still, there was no answer. She became worried so she backed up and sprang at the door, attempting to kick it down. It always looked so cool in movies. However, this was not a door on a set; it was real and very solid and did not budge against her extended leg. She rubbed her sore leg and called for backup anxiously, waiting outside of the apartment until another police officer, a strong muscular man in his mid-forties named Jose Martinez, showed up.

"Hey. Clara isn't answering the door. I tried knocking several times and I had news to share with her. I'm worried that she may be harmed or incapacitated," Officer Wilson explained to Officer Martinez.

"Okay. We'll find out what's going on," Officer Martinez reassured her.

He had a tool for picking locks with him and used it to unlock Clara's apartment door. The two police officers entered the apartment cautiously, both holding their guns in front of them, peering around the corner before passing further inside. Officer Martinez immediately started searching all the rooms and called Officer Wilson into the master bedroom.

She gasped audibly. She was still a fairly new police officer, only two years into her career, and she had only seen a handful of deaths in the line of duty. The sight of a dead body was devastating, especially the body of a woman she had known and sworn to protect. Officer Martinez rested his hand on her shoulder for a moment. He had been a police officer for much longer; he understood the devastation when you were still young and realized you couldn't protect everyone, no matter how hard you tried. Not that it ever got much easier. You just learned to cope.

Officer Wilson tried not to look, but it was hard not to stare at the gruesome sight. Clara's limbs were splayed across the king-sized bed. She was clutching a gun in her right hand. She had presumably shot herself in the head. The worst part was seeing the side of her head completely blown off. Pieces of skin, a pool of blood, and chunks of her brain lay on the pillow her head was resting on. She hadn't gone peacefully, but it had been quick. There was a note on the nightstand.

"It was suicide. She left a note," Officer Martinez said, pointing to the nightstand.

"We can't rule out homicide immediately. Someone planned Jackson's death and made it look like an accident. They could have set this up too."

"Her fiancé died tragically. I don't blame the poor girl."

"I don't know," Officer Wilson said, staring at the lifeless body on the bed. "What does the note say?"

She looked over his shoulder so she could read the barely legible handwriting and they read it at the same time.

I didn't want things to end this way, but I couldn't handle the guilt of setting up Jackson's death. I bought the bullets, I loaded the gun, and I wanted him to die. Once I found out how much debt he was in and that he wouldn't be able to pay all the money back, I was scared. I didn't want to marry him anymore. It was too late to back out of the proposal I had already accepted. It was what I had waited so long for and I didn't want everyone to know the embarrassing truth: I wanted Jackson because of his money. But I couldn't handle what I did to him. He didn't deserve to die. I loved him so much and now I can join him for eternity. Clara

"I guess you were right. I may have misjudged the situation," Officer Wilson said.

"We'll take this to forensics and confirm that this is her handwriting, test it for fingerprints, and then test the gun also. We will confirm that it was a suicide and then everyone will be able to rest safely, knowing Jackson's murderer is dead."

"I hope you're right," Officer Wilson said hesitantly.

"I've seen this type of situation before. Someone kills their spouse or lover, regrets it, then commits suicide. It happens more often than you would think."

"God, that's awful."

"Let's call this in. We better make sure everyone else involved with the case knows that Clara is dead now."

"Right."

Officer Martinez stepped into the sitting room to make the phone call, while Officer Wilson stayed in the bedroom, staring at Clara's body. She wasn't ready to accept Clara's death as a suicide. Something didn't add up. She had believed everything Clara told her. She had been so sure that Clara was innocent. How could she have been wrong about something like that? Were her instincts that far off? There had to be another explanation. If she was right, then there was someone else out there who had now been the cause of two deaths and they weren't random killings. Whoever the murderer was seemed intent on targeting Jackson and the people he was closest to. Officer Wilson thought the best thing to do was to interrogate Gus, the director of the TV show Jackson had been on, and to interrogate Edgar again. Maybe they could shed some light on the situation. She wondered how well either of them knew Clara and if either of them thought she was capable of murder.

Officer Wilson saw something blue sticking out from underneath the blanket by Clara's arm. She lifted the blanket and found a blue paracord bracelet. Maybe it was Clara's? She stared at the gawky, diamond engagement ring and diamond earrings Clara had adorned. She doubted the bracelet belonged to her; it wasn't her style. She quickly pocketed the bracelet and threw the blanket back over Clara.

"It's all taken care of," Officer Martinez called out from the hallway leading to the master bedroom.

"Okay," Officer Wilson responded, leaving the bedroom and joining him in the sitting room.

"We have to wait until the forensics team, the police captain, and detectives arrive," he said.

"Alright."

"You knew her, right? I mean, you talked to her before?"

"Yeah. I interrogated her about Jackson's death on two separate occasions and we met a few other times to discuss potential suspects and other aspects of the case."

"I'm sorry. I know how much harder it is when you know them personally. It's much worse than seeing a stranger's dead body."

"It's even worse because I promised she would be safe. I had officers stationed outside of her apartment every day for the past few weeks. It wasn't 24/7 though, since we've been so short-staffed and busy with other cases. I swore she would be okay. I never thought something would happen to her. She didn't deserve this," Officer Wilson said sorrowfully.

"Hey, it's okay. We will get it sorted out. Besides, right now we are treating this as a suicide. We have no reasonable evidence to make us believe it was a homicide."

"I don't think she was capable of murder."

"Technically, she didn't physically kill Jackson herself. She loaded the gun and planted it; someone else unknowingly pulled the trigger. She could have planned it that way, so she didn't have to get her hands dirty."

"That makes sense, but something feels wrong. Like it's a set-up."

"We need evidence if you want to prove that."

Officer Wilson's eyes suddenly lit up and she ran back into the bedroom to read Clara's suicide note again. "In her note, she said she was scared when she found out how much debt Jackson was in because he wouldn't be able to pay it all back. But that doesn't make sense. Clara didn't know about Jackson's debt until after he was killed. She didn't write this note and she didn't commit suicide."

Officer Martinez sighed. "I know you don't want to believe Clara was capable of murder, but it's the only reasonable explanation. Besides, you have no way of proving that Clara didn't know about Jackson's debt."

"My word isn't good enough?"

"You know it's not that simple, Delia."

"Yeah..." Officer Wilson responded in an aggravated tone. She was sick of arguing with Officer Martinez. She knew her instincts could be wrong, but she was sticking to what she believed. Besides, the bracelet...

The forensics team, detectives, and other police officers began filing into the apartment. They began compiling evidence while wearing white gloves, so nothing was tainted. There was police tape sectioning off the apartment now, so no one could wander in. Officer Wilson stood back and watched her colleagues at work. It was gratifying to know that their job was to uncover the truth and she knew none of them would stop until the case was solved. She trusted each of them, even the ones she didn't know as more than an acquaintance, simply because their chosen professions were similar. All these men and women gathered in this luxurious, expansive apartment in NYC were there because they believed in aiding the greater good.

Someone stepped over the police tape and fought his way into the apartment.

"Stop him!" One of the police officers yelled out.

"It's okay," Officer Wilson said, approaching the man. "I know him."

"What happened?" The man asked frantically, looking at the chaos in the apartment. "Is Clara okay?"

Officer Wilson reached out to touch the man on the shoulder. "I'm sorry, Edgar. Clara is dead."

Edgar stared back at her in disbelief. "She can't- it's not possible...how?" He stumbled over his words.

"I came over to talk to her. We had a meeting set up, but she wasn't answering the door, so I called for backup. We found her body in the master bedroom. It appears to be a suicide. I'm so sorry."

"God, why is this happening?" Edgar asked, pulling at his long dark hair, agitated, and continuing to wildly look around. "Wait, what do you mean 'it appears to be a suicide?'"

"Well, we found a suicide note on the nightstand, but we haven't matched it to her handwriting or tested it for fingerprints yet. If it was a suicide, that would mean Jackson's killer is dead and we could wrap up the case. But it seems rather odd that Clara would have chosen now to kill herself. Something isn't right."

"Hey, that's classified information you're revealing to a civilian," Officer Martinez said, stepping over to intrude on the conversation.

"He was friends with Clara and Jackson," Officer Wilson explained solemnly.

"I was coming over to watch a movie with her..." Edgar trailed off, holding up a copy of the *Lord of the Rings* trilogy on DVD.

"I'm sorry you had to find out like this, but no civilians are allowed behind police tape. This is a crime scene, so unfortunately I'm going to have to escort you out of here, but we'll be in touch," Officer Martinez said, walking Edgar to the door.

"I'll call you when we have more information," Officer Wilson said to Edgar. "We will want to talk with you again now that there has been another death connected to Jackson's murder."

"Of course, anything I can do to help," Edgar responded. "I can't believe it. Clara is gone..."

"I know. We will talk later, Edgar. I'm sorry you're going through this," Officer Wilson said sympathetically.

Edgar left and everyone else continued the investigation, trying to determine whether the suicide note was real, and if Clara's death had been of her own doing or someone else's. The truth would be discovered soon enough.

CHAPTER 29:
Edgar

Edgar threw a framed picture across the room, then seized a ceramic vase and threw that too. He wanted everything to shatter and break into dozens of tiny pieces. An hour ago, he had received a phone call from Maura, the director of *The Quest*. He hadn't gotten the main role of Lucas. Instead, he was offered a minor role with only a few scenes in the movie. He had politely declined and thanked Maura for the offer. But the second he was off the phone, he was all fury and rage, any trace of polite apology gone. He had been too cocky about the role. He had wanted it too badly, so it had been taken from him before it was his. It wasn't fair. First, he had lost Jackson, then the TV show he had been a part of for the past few years had ended, and now he couldn't even get a damn acting job that was worthy of his talent. He felt like he was losing everything. Soon there would be nothing left of him, only scattered pieces of what used to be a whole person.

It was funny how things never turned out the way you expected. He had no one left who cared about him, no one to show concern about his deteriorating state of mind and the loss he had suffered.

***

"What? Is this a joke? Do you hate us, Edgar?" His dad, Jerry, asked in horror, his eyes wide behind his glasses. He had long dark hair past his chin and dark brown eyes. Edgar eerily resembled his dad in looks, but not much else.

"Of course not. I'm telling you because I love you both and I wanted you to know who I really am."

"Well, your mother and I don't care to know about such things. Your lifestyle choices are…disappointing, to say the least."

"It's not a choice, Dad! I can't help it. I was born like this. Do you think I asked for it? Life is so much harder for me than most people. I can't outwardly express myself without people judging me or telling me I'm going to hell. No one would willingly choose such a difficult path."

His mom, Barbara, finally spoke up. "Edgar, sweetie, we will get you some help. You can talk to Father Thomas. They have places for people like you to get straightened out. Father Thomas will fix this." She smiled gently at Edgar and brushed her strawberry blonde hair behind her ears, although it was perfectly in place.

Edgar laughed harshly, throwing his hands up. "You guys never really gave a shit about me. I know you didn't want me. I was an accident and I ruined your otherwise perfect little lives."

"Edgar-" His mom attempted to interrupt him.

"No. It's the truth. I thought you would be more accepting because I'm your son and you're supposed to love me no matter what, but apparently you both didn't know that's what parents are supposed to do."

His dad stared at him coldly. "Fine. If you're going to act this way, we aren't going to be a part of it. If you aren't willing to change...if this is the life you've chosen for yourself, then you are no longer a member of this family."

"Dad, please..." Edgar said, choking back a sob and looking at his mom for help. She ignored him and buried her face into her husband's shoulder.

"You'll figure things out the hard way, Edgar. Maybe it will toughen you up and you'll realize you're making a mistake. Until then, you'll have to earn your own money and find a place to stay. Don't come back here. You are not my son anymore."

Edgar reflected on that moment and how it had destroyed him and shaped his future. Years later and still no one else knew. He couldn't bear experiencing the same rejection as he had with his parents. It wasn't worth it. He felt like a failure. What kind of life had he made for himself? Would his parents be proud of him now? He wondered offhandedly if they had watched *Dispatching David* and what they thought of the show. Edgar looked at the mess he had made in his apartment, turned off the light, and stumbled into his bedroom to get some sleep. The mess was a concern for another day. He had enough of today.

CHAPTER 30: Officer Wilson

Officer Wilson stared around the room, looking at the set pieces on *Dispatching David*. Gus had insisted on meeting at the location where the show was filmed, so she had obliged, willing to meet his demands if he would answer a few questions.

"How well did you know Jackson?" She asked when Gus finally showed up, 20 minutes after their mutually agreed upon time.

Gus sat in his director's chair and Officer Wilson pulled up a chair to sit across from him.

"I've known him since he got the lead role on the show, five years ago, so I would like to think I knew him pretty well. But we had a work relationship. I didn't know much about his personal life, besides the fact that he had a pretty little girlfriend who he was supposed to marry next year."

Officer Wilson typed furiously on her laptop. It was the best method for notetaking, in her opinion. "Did you know of any enemies in his life? Or someone who would want to hurt him? Was there anyone on the show who didn't like him?"

Gus paused, thinking for a minute before answering. "No, no. Everyone on the show liked him. But, like I said, I didn't know much about his personal life. I guess there could have been someone who wasn't involved in the show that would want to kill him."

Officer Wilson looked up from her laptop and stared curiously at Gus. "Why would someone want to kill Jackson? What would their motivation be for getting rid of him?"

"Oh, shit, I don't know. He was a celebrity; maybe there was a crazy fan who was in love with him or someone who hated the show. Who knows?"

"Do you know if he received a lot of fan mail? Or any threatening messages?"

"I have no idea, Officer Wilson. That would be a good question for his fiancée."

"You're right. It would be... Unfortunately, we discovered her body in her apartment yesterday afternoon."

"What? Is she...?"

"Yes, she's dead. There was a suicide note, claiming she killed Jackson, but we haven't finished investigating the crime scene to clarify that it was in fact a suicide."

"Damn. I didn't see that one coming... at first, I thought Jackson's death was some sort of freak accident, but this is insane. Why would Clara kill Jackson? She was head over heels for him."

"Did you ever see the two of them together? Did they seem

happy?"

Gus shrugged his shoulders and scratched the stubble on his chin. "I guess so. I wasn't around the two of them much. But they were going to get married. They must have been happy."

"Hmm. Jackson's friend Edgar is on the show too, correct?"

"Yeah. He actually took over Jackson's role to finish filming the last episode."

"He did? Was that his idea or yours? How do you think viewers of the show will react when they watch the last episode and see Jackson's character replaced with Edgar?"

Gus shook his head in an agitated manner. "There are always people who are upset about how things are handled when death is involved, especially for a tragedy like this one. There's not much we can do about that. We decided it was worth it to finish the show because the fans have waited so long to find out how it would end. We don't want to cheat them of the ending because of an untimely but senseless murder."

"You don't think the fans will be outraged that Jackson was replaced?"

"They may be, but we have invested so much time, work, and money into this show. It would be a shame to give up so close to the end. We were all incredibly horrified to witness Jackson's death, but precautions have been taken to ensure that a mistake of that magnitude will never happen again."

"Thank you for answering my questions, Gus. I appreciate you taking the time to talk to me about Jackson."

"No problem, and hey, if you ever need anything else, just let me know," Gus said with a wink, handing Officer Wilson a business card. "My number is on there. Feel free to call at any time." He winked again.

"Oh, um, thank you, sir," she stuttered, flustered, while rising from her seat and shaking his hand. She left hurriedly. She had never been especially good at dealing with the advances of males. Besides, she knew Gus was married and wasn't about to find herself in an uncomfortable situation.

Officer Wilson was walking down the sidewalk thinking about her conversation with Gus. If only she had thought of the idea sooner... then she could have asked Clara if she knew about any crazed fans. It was too late for that, but maybe Edgar would have some useful information. She hurried down the street. She was supposed to meet Edgar in a few hours, but she wanted to head back to the police station in between her meetings. She wanted to see if any new information had been discovered about the case.

When she arrived at the police station, it was a state of organized chaos as usual. She headed to her desk and checked her messages, powered on her computer, and checked in on the case. No new information had been discovered and it seemed clear that no one wanted to believe Clara's death was anything other than suicide. It made the entire ordeal easier to deal with. Clara had set up Jackson's death, couldn't live with the guilt, and then killed herself. It wrapped up the case like a perfectly wrapped present. There were no loose ends; no one was left wondering about the motivation for murder or worrying about interrogating other suspects. They could move on to the next case with everything settled. But Officer Wilson knew things were rarely that simple and she didn't think this was one of those times. Most of the other police officers were much older than her and much closer to retirement. She didn't want to wrongly assume things about them, but it seemed as if they had become lazy over the years and were constantly seeking simple solutions for complicated matters. It was easier if Clara had been the cause of all of this because that meant there wasn't a crazed murderer running around the city with some bloodthirsty motive for killing both Jackson and Clara. However, it didn't make sense for Clara to kill Jackson and then herself. Officer Wilson knew she was onto something. There were too many details in both murders that didn't make sense.

Officer Wilson stealthily pulled a file out of her desk drawer. The file contained information about the case which was highly classified. Technically, she had access to the file, but there was a formal process to view classified papers like this one. She didn't want anyone to know she was doing outside work on the case by herself. She flipped through the papers, not finding anything particularly astonishing. She sighed and closed the file, setting it on her desk.

"Whatcha got there?" A deep voice abruptly asked.

Officer Wilson jumped, startled. "Oh, geez, you scared me."

Jose laughed. "Sorry. I didn't mean to. What are you looking at? What file is that?" He asked, squinting to read the label on it.

"Um. It's the Birkman file," she said carefully.

"What? That case is done."

"No, it's not."

"Well, not officially, but close enough. We're closing it tomorrow unless new evidence comes in, but there would have to be sufficient proof for us to open the case back up." Jose picked up the file and tucked it under his arm. "You don't still think someone else set it up, do you?"

Officer Wilson tried not to glare at him. "I don't know," she said uncertainly, not knowing how much information she should reveal to him. He didn't seem to care what she thought.

"Hmm. Give it up, Officer. I know you want to believe the best about that girl, but everything we found points to her death being a suicide. It's best to let it go. We have plenty of other cases to work on. I'll have a new one on your desk tomorrow morning. Until then, I suggest you take your mind off things. Do you want to make a coffee run?"

Officer Wilson sighed exasperatedly. Everyone assumed that because she was a woman, she didn't mind making coffee runs all the time. Plus, it was so stereotypical of them to be drinking coffee. Next, they would be requesting her to drop by Krispy Kreme for donuts too. She refused to play into the stereotype. She was a strong minded, intelligent woman who was not going to give up on what she believed. She believed in justice, not placing blame on innocent parties. If there really was a murderer out there, she was going to make damn sure that they didn't get away with it. No. They would end up in prison if it was the last thing she did.

"Sure, yeah, I'll go get coffee," she finally responded.

"Thanks. The fresh air will be good for you," Officer Martinez said with a bright smile.

"Mhm," she said with a carefully concealed roll of her eyes.

CHAPTER 31:
Edgar

I can't believe Clara is gone," Edgar said with a tremble in his lip.

"This must be a very difficult time for you. I'm sorry, but it's best if the questioning is done now so we can close the case as soon as possible," Officer Wilson said. "The longer we wait, the harder it becomes for the evidence to hold up and to track down the murderer if it wasn't Clara."

"I know, I understand. It's just- you're right. It's a difficult time." He pushed his glasses up on his nose and tucked his long hair behind his ears. "I'm willing to answer your questions though. I want to help as much as I can."

"I spoke with Gus this morning. He revealed some interesting information that we didn't have before. I was wondering if you know about any obsessed fans Jackson may have had. Was anyone sending him lots of mail, crazed, or possibly stalking him?"

"He always had lots of fans and girls would go crazy when they saw him in public." He paused thoughtfully, resting his chin in his hand and suddenly lighting up with a realization. "Actually, yeah, he did have this one fan last year who began to threaten him. He was going to contact the police if it continued, but as soon as he warned her about getting authorities involved, she left him alone. Do you think she could be involved?" Edgar asked, wide-eyed.

"It's possible," Officer Wilson said cautiously, not wanting to divulge too much information as she accidentally had before to Clara. "Do you remember her name or any identifying information about this girl?"

"I think her name was...Sandra? She lived in NYC because I remember she said she liked to watch Jackson from outside of his apartment."

"Would these letters still be with Jackson's belongings?"

"They might be, but when his parents flew here for the funeral they went through his stuff. They took most of it with them, so if you can't find the letters you may want to speak with them."

"Okay, I can call them if necessary."

They sat in silence for a few minutes while Officer Wilson typed their conversation verbatim into a document on her laptop. Finally satisfied, she stopped typing and looked up at Edgar.

"Do you know anything else about Sandra?"

"Not really. Jackson only mentioned her a few times and he didn't like talking about it much because the situation freaked him out."

"Hmm. Alright. I'll look into it."

"Is there anything else you want to know?"

"You knew Jackson pretty well, correct?"

"Yeah, I've known him since we were in preschool. We grew up together, went to the same college, we were even roommates for a while."

"Do you think Clara would have any reason to want Jackson to die?"

Edgar stared at her quizzically. "I don't know..."

"You aren't sure? Is there something you need to tell me?"

"Look, Clara loved him despite their issues. And he loved her too." Edgar fidgeted in his chair, twisting his bracelet around his wrist.

"'Despite their issues?' Did they fight a lot?"

"What couple doesn't have their issues?" Edgar said, shrugging his shoulders. "Jackson refused to commit for years, Clara wanted a huge diamond engagement ring and an extravagant, over the top wedding... Jackson had some financial problems. He was never great at saving. Eventually, he decided he wanted to get married, she moved into his apartment, and they were happy. They had their differences, but they made it work."

"What made him change his mind about committing?"

"I suppose he realized he would lose her if he didn't make up his mind about marriage. Officer Wilson, I don't pretend to be an expert on relationships and I know Jackson didn't tell me everything that was going on."

"I have one more question to ask you before I let you leave." She paused, preparing herself for the answer.

"Did you kill Jackson Birkman?"

The Long Shadow on the Stage

CHAPTER 32:
Edgar

I can't believe camp is almost over. Next year we'll be too old to come back," Edgar said to Jackson as they packed their bags.

"I know. It's weird. But I won't miss going weeks without video games or TV," Jackson joked.

Edgar laughed. "Yeah."

"But, on the bright side, we can see PG-13 movies soon! You know what that means..."

"More graphic violence and swearing?"

"Well, yeah. But also..." Jackson looked around before continuing and leaned in closer to Edgar to whisper, "Boobs."

Edgar's face turned bright red at the word as he nervously giggled.

Jackson slapped him on the back. "Oh, come on. You know you can't wait. That will be the best part!"

"I don't know," Edgar said uncomfortably. "I don't really care about that stuff."

"It's not like super important," Jackson said. "It's just the next step of becoming a man."

"I thought becoming a man meant stepping up and being responsible..."

"That's part of it. But there's more than just that."

Edgar shyly turned away and fidgeted with his duffel bag.

"Oh, Edgar. You're so innocent," Jackson teased. "It's not bad, don't worry. I think it's cool that you don't care about certain things, like you don't try to fit in."

"I just try to be myself," Edgar said, adjusting his glasses. He had recently gotten new ones and they didn't quite fit his face. He had convinced his parents to let him keep his hair longer to look cooler, so his hair was in the in-between stage of growing out. He was in the prime of his awkwardness.

Meanwhile, Jackson had short spiky hair, no glasses, and was the tallest boy in their grade, so he was automatically popular. The factors that went into being popular in middle school weren't an exact science, but Edgar was popular simply by association.

"I respect that, dude."

The two boys continued packing and they fell into the comfortable silence that only two people who are very close can share. Jackson was essentially throwing his clothes into his Nike duffel bag, not caring if his shirts were wrinkled by the trip, whereas Edgar was carefully folding each clothing item before placing it in his duffel bag. Edgar pulled something out of his duffel bag and held it in his open palm for Jackson to see.

"I made these for us," Edgar said, waiting for Jackson to look at the bracelets he was holding.

They were identical paracord bracelets; one was blue and the other was black. Edgar had made them in the arts section of camp on the day when Jackson had chosen to learn how to canoe.

"Thanks, man," Jackson said, taking the blue bracelet and tying it around his wrist. He held his arm out and looked at it. "Cool."

"I made them so we remember that we will always be friends, no matter what," Edgar said.

Jackson nodded. "I know we will be. No one else will put up with me," he said, laughing obnoxiously.

"Probably true," Edgar said, smiling and going back to his packing.

"Hey, Edgar?" Jackson said after several minutes of silence while they were finishing their packing.

"Yeah?"

"Is there…is there a reason why you don't uh- why you don't like boobs?"

"WHAT?" Edgar practically shouted in astonishment.

"Sorry, that came out wrong. I mean, I'm not going to hate you if you don't like girls. I won't judge you."

"Jackson, I don't know why you would even think that! Of course it's not true and I'm not discussing this with you anymore." Edgar turned back to his duffel bag, although he was done packing, and pretended to arrange his clothing, hiding his red face and shaking hands from his best friend. He didn't know why, but he didn't want Jackson to know the truth.

The Long Shadow on the Stage

CHAPTER 33: Officer Wilson

The handwriting in Clara's supposed suicide note didn't match her writing. It was close, but upon closer inspection looked too different to be confirmed as hers. The writing in the note was compared to several handwritten notes Clara had jotted down at work. Officer Wilson felt sick when this was discovered. Someone had framed Clara for Jackson's death, then killed her. She couldn't believe how twisted people could be. What could possibly have happened to make someone go to such lengths? Revenge? Money? What was it about Jackson that had been so awful that he deserved to die? Officer Wilson pondered this until she realized something else. If they had killed Clara also, maybe she had known too much and they had to shut her up. Maybe Clara had figured out who killed Jackson. If the suicide note hadn't been written by her, then who had gone through all this trouble to make it look like a suicide? Someone who was deadset on not getting caught, that was certain.

"I knew I wasn't crazy," she told Jose as they pored over the file for what felt like the hundredth time, trying to piece together all the clues they had found. "I never thought it was Clara who switched the guns. There wasn't a strong enough motive. After getting to know her, I didn't think she was capable of murder."

Jose nodded. "I know, I never thought so either."

Officer Wilson chuckled. "Yeah, okay. Sure you did. Anyways, I remembered there was a private detective who helped Jackson when he was kidnapped. His name was Jerry Walden. I thought he could be helpful because clearly this entire case is out of our league. We need outside help."

"We have a detective who has been investigating the case already," Jose said, irritated. "We don't need anyone else involved. That's how classified information gets compromised."

"I understand that, but I think we could use a fresh perspective. We are too close to the case, especially me. We all have too much invested in it. If we brought in Jerry, he might find something we're overlooking. I really think he can help."

"Oh, fine. You're lucky you're pretty," Jose said with a smirk.

Officer Wilson ignored the comment and turned back to the file. She didn't think as highly of Jose after their first date when he had tried to sleep with her. Their date had been a few months ago, but she wasn't the kind of person who slept around and was offended that he assumed she would after one mediocre date. Since then, things had been awkward between them as they tried to navigate their entwining work lives without becoming too personal. She supposed it would have been smart if she had never agreed to the date in the first place. Dating a co-worker opened too many undesirable possibilities.

Just then, Jerry Walden walked into the police station and came over to them, introducing himself to Officer Martinez.

"Nice to meet you," Jerry said politely, extending his hand to Officer Martinez. "I was sad to hear about Jackson's death. I'm the one who helped him get to safety the day he was kidnapped. He was in bad shape that day. Even though I barely knew him, I was worried about him. He seemed like he was in trouble. Maybe drugs or money problems."

"How do you know that? Did he tell you?" Officer Martinez asked snidely.

"No, it was the vibe I got from the situation. I mean, he was knocked unconscious and kidnapped, then murdered on the set of his TV show soon afterwards. Doesn't it seem like something shady was going on?"

"I think you're right. I don't know if drugs had anything to do with it, but Jackson did have issues with finances, which could be related to his death. His friend Edgar was loaning him money for quite some time," Officer Wilson said.

Jerry nodded sagely. "I thought so. Was he a gambler?"

"I'm not sure. He obviously owed lots of money to someone. He said Jackson was never good at saving and that he liked to spend money faster than he could earn it. He owned several expensive cars and had a huge luxury apartment on the Upper East Side."

"Sounds like a classic case of someone who borrowed money and couldn't afford to pay it back. He must have made a deal with someone and they decided they wanted the money back sooner than planned. When he couldn't pay it, they killed him."

"Why would they go through such an elaborate plan to set up Clara? Don't people like that usually just kill the person in debt and leave their body in the streets?" Officer Martinez asked.

"Sometimes. He may have bought the cars from outside of a dealership and couldn't afford the payments. If they were from an outside party, they could have killed him when they didn't get their money," said Jerry.

Officer Martinez laughed loudly. "This is ridiculous. You two can keep chattering about these theories as much as you want, but we have no reason to believe he was involved in some shady deal. I say we keep letting the detective currently involved with the case work on it and see what they uncover. They already know all the details."

Jerry held his hand up respectfully. "I understand why you don't like me, Officer. However, I saw Jackson the day he was kidnapped. He was beaten up badly. Officer Wilson saw him too, so she can vouch for me."

"He's right, Jose. We need to find out where he bought his cars and see if they were paid off, then we can go from there."

"Fine. I'll have no part of this. I want to let the professionals do their job. I'm staying out of it."

"That's your decision and it's perfectly understandable," Jerry said complacently. "This line of investigation isn't for everyone. Some people can't handle it."

Jose snorted in contempt and stomped off to the breakroom.

Officer Wilson turned to Jerry. "And I deal with that on a daily basis," she said with a sigh.

Jerry laughed good-naturedly. "Don't worry about him. He

seems like the sort who has to be right and when he doesn't get his way, it's the end of the world. Now let's go find out where Jackson bought his fancy cars."

The Long Shadow on the Stage

CHAPTER 34:
Blaine

Blaine found out about Clara's death while watching the news in the morning as he was getting ready for work. He was pouring milk into his bowl of Cheerios when he saw Clara's face appear on the TV screen. The volume was muted, but next to Clara's face there was a photo of Jackson Birkman, her dead fiancé. On the screen flashed the words, *Case wrapped up as police confirm Clara Rogers killed Jackson Birkman after he lost all his money, then she later committed suicide.*

Blaine dropped the half gallon of milk and it splashed onto the table, spilling onto the kitchen floor, but he didn't care. Clara had stood him up for their date over the weekend. He was hurt about the situation, but he had assumed things were moving too fast for Clara and that she backed out because she wasn't ready to start dating again. He understood and had been doing his best to give her space the last few days. He didn't want to rush into things and lose her. Although, the fact that he hadn't been able to get ahold of her had begun to worry him.

There was no way Clara had killed Jackson or committed suicide. It made no sense. She seemed so happy with him and she finally had everything she wanted after he proposed. Why would she kill him? And had Jackson really lost all his money? It seemed insane; he couldn't believe the case involved someone he knew and cared about, much less that she had set up Jackson's death. He decided he wouldn't go in to work today. He couldn't handle Clara's absence at the desk near his own. It was too much to bear, especially since they had gotten closer lately. As Clara had begun to heal from the loss of Jackson, Blaine had thought he finally stood a chance of winning her over. Even after Blaine thought Clara had stood him up, he still thought they would make it work eventually. But he could worry about his lost chance at love later. Right now, what was more important was figuring out who would set up Clara for Jackson's death. Who was responsible and how could he help prove Clara had no part in this horrible affair?

CHAPTER 35: Officer Wilson

Officer Martinez approached Officer Wilson's desk at the police station and stood in front of it until she noticed him. She was busily scanning through documents on her laptop and it took her a moment to realize he was standing by her desk.

"Oh! Sorry," she said, suddenly looking up.

"It's fine," he said, smiling dazzlingly at her, crossing his arms over his chest and leaning back against her desk.

"Do you have more information about the case?" She asked.

"Not yet unfortunately, although I guess I was wrong about the case being closed today. I thought the Captain would confirm it was done, but he thinks there is more to it."

"Really? That's great news! Then I'll continue working on it with his permission," she said excitedly. Now she wouldn't have to go behind his back to keep investigating.

"I actually had something else to talk to you about. It's not work related."

"Oh?" She said, only half-listening. She wanted to solve the damn case and find out the truth. It was important to her because she had been personally involved in the case since the beginning, even before the two deaths. In part, she knew she was responsible for what had happened. She should have been more careful, tried harder to protect Jackson and Clara. Maybe if she had done something differently, they would both still be alive.

Officer Martinez smiled warmly. "I was wondering if you would like to go on a date with me this Saturday."

"What?" She asked, her eyes widening as she stared at him, trying to gage if he was joking.

"Don't look so shocked! I know we went out once before, but I feel badly about the way things ended. I would like a chance to prove I'm not the kind of man you think I am," He said, grabbing her hand and stroking it gently. Officer Wilson immediately yanked her hand away.

Delia Wilson was a beautiful woman, who happened to receive lots of admiration and attention, mostly unwanted, from men of all ages. She didn't respond well to compliments. In fact, it had been quite some time since she had dated someone because she was focused on her career. Or at least that was her most frequently used excuse for declining dates.

"I don't know. I'm busy with the case. I don't have much free time. It makes it difficult to date. I'm sure you understand," she replied, not making eye contact with him.

"Are you telling me you're not interested? Because if that's true, then I'll leave you alone. But if you have even the slightest interest, don't leave me in the dark. Please."

"I don't think so. We already tried before and it didn't work out. I don't want to make our work relationship more strained than it has been lately."

"*Strained?*"

Officer Wilson looked directly at him. "I'm sorry, Jose," she said and turned her attention back to the stack of paperwork on her desk.

"Fine. I thought it was worth giving us another chance, but clearly I misjudged the situation."

"Clearly."

***

Jerry and Officer Wilson discovered that Jackson had in fact purchased his cars from an outside party, one that was no longer in business, perhaps partly because of Jackson neglecting to pay off any of his three extravagant cars, worth at least $1 million. It was difficult to track down the owner of the automotive business because he had left town after his business went under, leaving no trace except his mountains of debt. It was a dead end, they soon found out. After they finally found the man who had sold Jackson the cars, he showed them the payments Jackson had made over the past few years. Every month depicted Jackson paying his car loans on time, although he had outstanding debt on each one. But at least they knew Jackson hadn't purchased his cars from a dealer and the man who had sold him the cars hadn't played a part in his death. Billy was a fragile man in his late seventies who had a live-in nurse and resided in a tiny ground story apartment.

"I stopped selling cars a few months back," he explained to

Jerry and Officer Wilson. "I'm not as energetic as I used to be and it was becoming too difficult to keep track of the business. The real push to retire, though, was being diagnosed with lung cancer."

Jerry and Officer Wilson shared a solemn look.

"I'm sorry. That must be tough to deal with," Jerry responded.

"All those years of smoking, you know. I've always been a fighter, but this may just do me in," Billy said with a laugh, which turned into a coughing fit. "I'm sorry I can't be more help to the two of you." He weakly raised a glass of water to his lips, shaking as he did so.

"You've helped enough. Now we know why Jackson was in debt."

"Jackson was such a nice young man. He was so friendly and always made his car payments on time. I wish all my customers had been like him."

"We appreciate you taking the time to talk with us, sir," Officer Wilson said. "I only wish Jackson had been able to pay off his debt to you."

"Don't worry about me, Officer. I'll be fine. Jackson wasn't the only one up to his ears in car payments."

Officer Wilson felt badly for Billy and all suspicion vanished after talking with him. However, once again, they seemed to be pointing fingers at the wrong people. It was uncanny how they kept creeping closer and closer to the true criminal yet couldn't seem to pin them down.

Officer Wilson was exhausted, but still determined to fulfill her duty. She had vowed to protect human life and since she had failed in the case of Clara and Jackson, she would never be able to forgive herself. The best she could do was find out who had caused this awful series of events before they toyed with the police and detectives even more. Whoever it was had carefully planned out every detail. It hadn't been a spontaneous decision; it had probably taken months to set up. Whoever it was probably thought they were safe now. But, Officer Wilson was not giving up hope. Not yet. Because when you lose hope, what is left besides bitterness and disappointment?

She and Jerry continued to discuss every clue they had uncovered, hoping to find a new perspective that had been overlooked the first time. In a last-ditch effort to discover something new, they went to Jackson and Clara's apartment, this time with the clearance of the police captain. However, as it turned out, the inside of the apartment was the wrong place to look for clues. As they entered the hallway leading to Jackson and Clara's apartment, an elderly woman waddled towards her own apartment. She stopped and looked at them and beckoned them over.

"I remembered something else about that young man," Mrs. Dell said to the police officer and detective.

"What young man?" Jerry asked kindly. She seemed like a confused older woman.

"The one who was walking by Jackson's apartment." She looked at Officer Wilson. "I told you before he had long hair and haunting eyes, but I remembered something else. He was wearing glasses."

"Ma'am, I've never met you before...who are you talking about?" Officer Wilson asked in anticipation.

"Why, aren't you the young lady whose cat was killed?" Mrs.

Dell asked, peering at her over her old-fashioned circular glasses.

"No, I'm Officer Wilson."

"Oh, my! I thought you were Jackson's girlfriend. You look so alike it's uncanny! I'm sorry to bother you, Officer," Mrs. Dell said, unlocking the door of her apartment.

"No, wait!" Officer Wilson said, stopping Mrs. Dell from entering her apartment. "You saw someone walk by Jackson's apartment on the day that Clara's cat was killed?"

"Yes, and I talked to her about it. She was very upset and in such a hurry she knocked me over! She was rather rude about the whole thing. She didn't even help me up," she huffed. "No respect. That's the trouble with those millennials. Anyways, I have to go. My husband is waiting for dinner. Nice talking with you," Mrs. Dell said, smiling, and starting to shut her apartment door.

"Excuse me, but could you repeat what you said about the man who was at the apartment that day?"

Mrs. Dell sighed loudly. "This is the last time I'll say it and then I really must get dinner going," she insisted. "The day Jackson's girlfriend knocked me over, I saw a young man in the hallway near Jackson's apartment. I was carrying in my groceries by myself and my husband was napping, so I didn't have anyone to help me with the heavy things as usual. But this nice young man came over and helped me. That was it. Have a nice day," Mrs. Dell said, beginning to pull her apartment key out of her purse.

"I apologize, ma'am, but what did this young man look like?"

Mrs. Dell frowned. "I already told you. He had long hair and glasses. And those eyes," she said, pausing. "His eyes were haunting."

CHAPTER 36:
Edgar

Edgar received dozens of angry letters, postcards, and Facebook messages in the days that passed after the last episode of *Dispatching David* aired on TV. It felt like everyone in America hated him for replacing Jackson in the show. He justified his actions to himself, but there was only so much he could do to convince everyone else. Gus had publicly announced that the show would culminate with Edgar Peterson in David's role and everyone had revolted. It was a miracle the TV station hadn't pulled the show, but they had already finished filming it and didn't want to waste the money that had gone into the series finale. Of course, it was always about the money as far as TV stations were concerned.

He watched the episode live while alone in his apartment. He didn't have anyone to watch it with and it seemed strange to not have Jackson with him. They had hosted their own little viewing party each week, admiring their shining moments and mocking themselves onscreen when they mangled the scene or deviated from the script at all. They always split a six pack of beer and Clara would yell at Jackson for drinking on a weeknight because no matter how many times he did it, she never accepted it and he never seemed to care. But it wasn't the same watching it without Jackson there. This time Edgar drank a six pack by himself and cried hysterically as the beginning credits rolled. Jackson's name appeared on the screen with the words "In Loving Memory" before it.

The ending was perfect. He had finally acted in a great role where millions had watched him, but he didn't have his best friend to enjoy it with him, so why did it matter? If he had no one to enjoy it with, the success wasn't as great as he had imagined. He always thought Jackson would be beside him when his acting talent was finally recognized. Plus, Gus hadn't followed through with his grand promise of getting him a role in the upcoming Anne Hathaway movie. Edgar was bitter about the broken promise, but it hadn't been exactly what he wanted so it wasn't the end of the world. It had been his dream to be on Broadway ever since he was six and saw a production of *Phantom of the Opera,* so he would find another road to success, one that wasn't full of potholes, roadkill, and unclear road markers.

CHAPTER 37: Officer Wilson

Officer Wilson knew there had to be more to Jackson's financial issues than the troubles with making his car payments on his luxury cars, overextending himself on rent, and buying nice presents for Clara. Or was it as simple as Jackson never quite learning how to manage his finances? Had Jackson been that irresponsible with his money? He did come from a wealthy family, with parents who spoiled him and gave him everything he wanted. He never had to work for anything until his parents cut him off and he moved to NYC. Officer Wilson supposed that sometimes celebrities who suddenly became wealthy adjusted their lifestyle to match their new salary, without considering saving or investing money for emergencies, therefore squandering their money away on their extravagant parties, top shelf liquor, and private jets.

Edgar had admitted Jackson was borrowing money from him for years. It still didn't quite make sense that Edgar would loan such a large amount of money to Jackson, even if they had been best friends for most of their lives. Officer Wilson knew her best bet was to try talking to Edgar again and see if he would divulge any more information. She was willing to bet that he knew more than he originally led her to believe. Besides, if Edgar really was his best friend, he probably knew all of Jackson's deepest darkest secrets. She just had to find a way to make Edgar reveal them.

This time they were meeting at the police station in the interrogation room. It was a much more formal meeting than their previous meetings, in part because Officer Wilson was becoming desperate and Edgar was her best chance of uncovering new information.

Edgar arrived fifteen minutes early, proving once again that he was the promptest person to exist.

"Officer Wilson," he said, cordially, shaking her hand as he entered the room.

"Nice to see you again, Edgar. Please, have a seat," she gestured at the empty chair across from hers.

Edgar sat and folded his hands in front of him on the cold metal table, staring at Officer Wilson and waiting for her to begin the questioning.

Officer Wilson flipped through her notepad. "So, you told me before that you were loaning Jackson money."

Edgar nodded.

"Do you know how much money you loaned him?"

Edgar paused in thought. "Several hundred thousand dollars. At least. I would have to check my financial statements for the exact amount."

Officer Wilson nodded. That lined up with what she had uncovered. "That is quite a large sum of money. Do you know what Jackson was using it for?"

Edgar shrugged his shoulders and adjusted his glasses. "Clara liked being spoiled. Jackson had a rather expansive apartment and a few expensive cars. He never thought about the future or planned for anything in his future. My guess is his money just ran out and I was his back-up plan so he could continue the lifestyle he and Clara had grown accustomed to."

Officer Wilson wrote furiously in her notebook. So far everything Edgar said he had either told her previously or she had guessed based on what she knew of Jackson's personality, as well as what she had uncovered during her research and thorough study of Jackson's financial records. "What was your relationship like with Jackson?" She suddenly asked, putting down her pen and looking Edgar directly in the eyes.

"Wh-what? Why do you need to know that?" Edgar stammered.

Officer Wilson smiled tightly. She had finally caught him off guard. "This is a murder investigation, Edgar, and the culprit hasn't been caught. Asking one of the people Jackson was closest to what their relationship was like with him isn't illogical."

"Right. Of course not," Edgar quickly responded. "Our relationship was…strong. We were friends since we were toddlers. We grew up together, went to summer camp together, attended the same college, discovered our passion for acting and auditioned for plays together, and both decided to leave our small hometown in Minnesota to move to NYC. I would have done anything in the world for Jackson." Edgar pursed his lips. "I can't necessarily say the same for Jackson because he could be extremely selfish at times, but he tried his best to be a good friend."

"What do you mean by that exactly? 'He tried his best?' How was he selfish?"

"I'm sure you understand, Officer Wilson. All friendships have one friend who is more selfish and entitled and the other who would sacrifice everything."

"Hmm," Officer Wilson said, tapping her pen against her lips. "Can you give a specific example?"

Edgar unfolded his hands and placed them neatly in his lap. "For example, after Jackson had been dating Clara for a while, he started spending more and more time with her. We spent less time together as a result."

"I don't understand. How was that selfish of him to spend time with his girlfriend?"

Edgar sighed heavily and ran his hands through his long dark hair, which shone multi-toned in the fluorescent lights. "Clara wasn't good for him. She cared too much about his success, fame, and money. Granted, she did start dating him before he was famous and wealthy, but still. She didn't always have his best interests at heart-"

"And you did?"

Edgar's eyes narrowed. "Of course."

"Just to clarify, you didn't know if Jackson was in any sort of trouble, did you?"

"What sort of trouble?"

"Other than his exorbitant amount of debt and unpaid bills,

was anything else going on?"

"I didn't want to say anything before, but I always wondered if Sandra's kid was Jackson's. I'm sure you interrogated her also, but if not, you may want to speak with her."

"Do you think Jackson was paying off Sandra to keep her quiet about his illegitimate child?"

"If Jackson did, in fact, have an affair with Sandra, then yes, I believe he would have paid her off and done everything else within the realm of possibility to ensure no one else ever found out."

"If you and Jackson were so close, wouldn't he have told you a secret like that?"

Edgar smiled sorrowfully. "Jackson knew how I felt about affairs and about Sandra. If he did sleep with her, he certainly wouldn't have told me about it."

***

Officer Wilson slammed her fist down on her desk and the other officers turned to look at her curiously. No one knew how much she cared about the case besides Jose and even he didn't fully understand why it bothered her that Clara's death was still labeled as a suicide. Since the case had remained open, she was left in an endless loop of wondering what she was missing in the set-up. Maybe there was one more clue, something that could prove she was right. The receipt hadn't proved anything because the purchase of the bullets had been made in cash. The surveillance footage at the store had been destroyed and the figure in the video had their face covered anyways. The old car dealership that Jackson owed a large outstanding debt to had also been a dead end, although now the source of most of his debt was cleared up. None of the evidence was enough to prove anything about Jackson's and Clara's deaths. Officer Wilson decided she would scour Jackson's and Clara's apartment one last time. If she didn't find anything new, she would stop searching and give up on the case.

She arrived in the apartment ten minutes later; it was close to the police station, so it had only been a short walk, although it was below freezing and she half-sprinted almost the entire way. Officer Wilson stepped over the caution tape and entered the master bedroom cautiously, not wanting to make her presence known if someone came back for an unexpected final sweep of the crime scene. The furniture was still there, but little else. The once lavish apartment appeared rather forlorn and weary, stripped away of the human essence that had once resided within its walls. The suicide note was gone, as was Clara's body, leaving little to inspect. She stared futilely at the bed, wishing a magical clue would suddenly appear to help her solve the case. The expensive looking comforter on the bed had blood stains splashed across it, which Officer Wilson inspected closely. The pillow had been completely drenched by the gunshot to the head. She walked over to the other side of the bed and lifted back the comforter. There was another pillow, which apparently hadn't been deemed important during the investigation. However, on the pillow, there lay several long, dark, scraggly hairs.

She knew it wasn't enough. Besides, she could still be wrong at this point. She needed to find Jackson's old fan letters to see if any of them were incriminating against the girl, Sandra, who had threatened him. She scoured the bedroom for papers or notes mentioning Sandra. She searched under the bed, in the dresser drawers, and finally in the closet, where she discovered a small stack of papers on the top shelf. They must have been overlooked by Jackson's parents when they were sorting through Jackson's belongings. Officer Wilson pulled down the loose papers and began rifling through them. Enclosed in the pile, there was a variety of letters: some were old love letters from Clara, a few letters Jackson's parents had mailed him during college presumably, and at the very bottom there were a few shorter letters from a girl named Sandra. Officer Wilson read the first one.

My dearest Jackson,

I am writing to you in hopes that I can meet you in person. I have tried waiting outside of your apartment a few times, but I always either lose my nerve about approaching you or you aren't around when I stop by. I wish you could understand how deeply I love you and that you are the only one I want to be with, now and forever. I will continue to wait for you until you realize you want me too.

Your true love,

Sandra

Officer Wilson set the letter aside, intending to bring it to the police station along with any other letters she uncovered. Perhaps the next one would be more revealing of Sandra's stalking, violent nature as Edgar had told her.

Jackson,

This will be my last letter to you as I have grown sick of waiting. I know I promised I would wait forever, but this game you're playing with me has grown old. I can't do this any longer. I know your girlfriend knows about me and she isn't happy about us.

I'm sorry for any trouble I may have caused and I hope you have a long, happy life without me in it.

    Sandra

    Jackson had written on the letter, *"October 12th, 2012 Sandra stopped by the apartment and I answered the door, not knowing who she was. As soon as she revealed her name, I immediately realized it was the girl who had been sending me creepy letters for months. I tried shutting the door, but she fought her way in and tried to convince me to have sex with her. When I refused, she threw a ceramic vase at my head. I called the police and they told me to keep a record of any more incidents that occurred."*

    Officer Wilson set the second letter on top of the first one and pondered the contents. If Jackson had called the police after the altercation with Sandra, there would be a record of it at the police station. Then she should be able to find Sandra's contact information and interrogate her about her rocky past with Jackson. She placed the letters in a binder containing other information from the case, then plucked the hairs from the pillowcase while wearing gloves and placed them in a small Ziploc bag.

    She left the apartment and headed back to the police station, hurrying along because the wind had picked up and the snow was coming down fiercer than before. The snow whirled around the sidewalks, blowing gusts around her as she walked. She regretted not taking a cab, but it seemed like a waste of money since the police station was only a few blocks away. The flakes fell heavy and fast, making the sidewalks slick. She wasn't paying attention, and, in her haste, she slid and fell on her butt. Her binder flew out of her hands and she scrambled to pick it up, ensuring that the contents remained safely tucked away. Once this fact was verified, Officer Wilson continued her walk back to the police station at a slightly slower, more careful pace. She entered the warmth of the police station in relief and shivered as she waited to warm up.

"Hey, where were you?" Officer Martinez asked, approaching her desk.

"I stepped out for a few minutes."

"Oh?"

"Yeah. Coffee run. I always need more caffeine midday," she said, laughing nervously. She was terrible at lying and she happened to hate coffee.

"Where's your coffee then? You should have gotten me some!" He joked.

"I drank it on the way back. It's snowing pretty hard now," she said, changing the subject clumsily.

"Yeah, I heard it's supposed to get bad later. There's a winter weather advisory or blizzard warning or some shit."

"I may have to catch a cab home. Usually I walk. I only live a few blocks away. I don't own a car," she explained, feeling like she was rambling.

"I can give you a ride home if you want. You shouldn't be outside for long in this weather anyways. All it takes is thirty minutes of being exposed and you can get frostbite," Jose said authoritatively.

"Thanks, that would be great. Well, I better get back to work then. I have a lot to get done today."

Jose nodded in agreement. "Me too. I just wanted to see what you were up to. Let me know when you're clocking out and I'll drive you home."

"Sure," she said, as Jose returned to his own desk.

Officer Wilson sighed in relief as he left and opened her binder. She pulled up the record of Jackson Birkman in the computer system and scrolled back to the year 2012. There were two items filed under that year. She opened them both and proceeded to read the files. The first one seemed to be the situation Jackson had written down on the letter from Sandra. The date matched the one he had transcribed. The second file, however, detailed another altercation with Sandra, which had happened after the first one. It described Jackson encountering Sandra on the sidewalk in front of his apartment one evening. She threw herself at him, demanding that he love her, otherwise she threatened to tell the police he had beaten her. The file went on to say that when Jackson had refused repeatedly, Sandra had threatened to kill him. She began hitting him and pulled out a knife. Jackson was able to stop her but called the police to ensure the incident was documented in case something further happened. The police had questioned Sandra, but no further action had been taken.

Officer Wilson sighed and ran her hands through the ends of her hair, mindlessly checking for split ends as she always did when she was agitated. Sandra had threatened Jackson, but other than maybe getting in a few punches, she had never physically harmed him. In addition to that, the incidents had all happened over three years ago, so it was little to go on. Sandra may be living somewhere else now or her contact information may not have been updated. Either way, there was potential for things to be difficult, but she was determined to track Sandra down.

***

As she stood outside of the cafe, she thought about how strange it was that she was interrogating someone for a murder case. She had never thought herself capable of dealing with seeing dead bodies and other gruesome sights or interrogating people about such touchy subjects. Before Officer Wilson had entered the police academy, she had imagined protecting people above all else because human life was precious and she hadn't believed that anyone was inherently evil. Everyone was a victim of their environment, whether cruel or kind, it impacted how individuals turned out and what they became as they grew into adults. The longer she worked as a police officer, however short a time it had been, she disagreed more and more with the viewpoints of humanity she had once held so dear. Now she knew the truth: there was evil everywhere and horrible acts were committed each day, but knowing this only made her want to protect people and uphold her morals and values even more. She had sworn to do her best to be a moral police officer, to serve the people and keep them safe. She intended on keeping that promise in any way she could, even if it meant digging around behind her boss's back a tad. He hadn't seen Clara's face as she wept over Jackson's death or talked to Jackson and Clara and known them as she had. To everyone else on the case, they were simply bodies, not real people. Officer Wilson had to admit sometimes that line of thinking made it easier to handle the senseless deaths, but it still didn't make it right.

After a few minutes of waiting outside, the cold became unbearable and Officer Wilson strode into the small but welcoming café to warm up. She ordered a large hot chocolate with extra whipped cream and found a bistro table in a quiet corner. A woman with frizzy brown hair and rectangular glasses approached her table.

"Are you Officer Wilson?" She asked.

"Yes. Sandra?"

"Yeah."

"Have a seat." Officer Wilson gestured at the chair across from her.

"I didn't kill Jackson, if that's what you think. I know you're probably going to ask me that, so I wanted to tell you upfront. I didn't do it. I haven't seen Jackson in years. I'm married now," Sandra said, holding up her left hand so her slim, gold wedding band was evident.

"Okay," Officer Wilson said slowly. She wasn't used to people taking charge of the situation when she was interrogating them. Sandra had jumped into the conversation before she could even ask her first question. She needed to stay in control of the conversation. "When was the last time you saw Jackson Birkman?"

"I told you I haven't seen him in years. Like, three years ago."

Officer Wilson scribbled down the information.

"Are you gonna write down everything I say?" Sandra asked, curiously peering over the notebook to try to read what she was writing.

"Yes. I like to keep a record of every conversation regarding the case."

"How thorough," Sandra said unexpectedly.

"Indeed," Officer Wilson responded, intrigued about Sandra's involvement with Jackson. After getting to know Clara, Sandra didn't seem like the type of woman Jackson would be interested in, much less have an affair with.

"So, what else do you wanna ask me? Ask away," Sandra said. "Actually, I need something to drink. I'll be right back."

Officer Wilson watched as Sandra ordered an iced coffee and she returned to the table several minutes later with her drink.

"Sorry. I don't care much for real coffee. Well, like, black coffee. But this stuff is pretty good," she said, sipping her iced coffee noisily.

"It's alright. Anyways, back to Jackson. What happened the last time you saw him?"

Sandra sighed obnoxiously and blew her long bangs off her forehead. "I really don't remember. That was a long time ago. I have my own family to worry about now."

"I looked up the file and it says here that in one reported altercation, you hit Jackson repeatedly and pulled out a knife. He tried to calm you down, then you threatened to kill him." Officer Wilson slid the file across the table so Sandra could read it too.

Sandra snorted after scanning the file. "Everyone has their own version of the truth, don't they? Jackson had a way of twisting things. That's why I finally gave up on him. He kept promising me he would leave his stupid little girlfriend, but he never did. He liked stringing me along."

"You were...involved with Jackson?" Officer Wilson asked.

"Well, yeah," Sandra said, as if it was obvious. "Every time his girlfriend was gone, I would go over to his apartment and have sex with him. He was great in bed, but not good at much else."

Officer Wilson smiled. "He was the lead actor on an award-winning TV show. I would venture to say he was good at that as well."

Sandra laughed nastily. "The show wasn't that great."

"How long did you have a relationship with Jackson?"

"Probably about…five months or so. Something like that," Sandra said, nodding as if in agreement with herself.

"Alright. So, what happened the day Jackson called the police? Do you mind telling me?" Officer Wilson asked gently, not wanting to push Sandra, but needing more information.

"Sure. I was at his place, like usual, and his girlfriend was supposed to be home soon, so he started going nuts and telling me I had to leave before she got home. I was upset because I wanted him to break up with her like he kept telling me he would." She slurped her iced coffee. "But he kept freaking out, so I told him if he didn't leave her that day, then I would kill him. I had a knife on me, yeah, but I didn't hurt him."

"You told Jackson you would kill him if he didn't leave Clara?"

"That's what I just said, isn't it?"

Officer Wilson stared at her notebook, reading what she had written. Something didn't add up. "How did you meet Jackson?"

Sandra smiled. "I was an extra on an episode of *Dispatching David*. I started talking to him one day because I thought he was cute. He seemed interested, so I thought we had something special going on, until I found out he had a girlfriend and he was a lying cheater." She slurped continuously at the last few drops of her drink for what seemed like forever to Officer Wilson, until she finally decided her iced coffee was gone.

"Okay. And I can verify this if I check with Gus?"

"What? You don't believe me?" Sandra asked, her eyes narrowing.

"I think I have enough information, Sandra. Thank you for taking the time to talk to me." She shook her hand and Sandra limply returned the favor.

"Fine, if that's all you wanted. Seems like a waste of time to me. And good riddance about Jackson dying. He was an asshole and he deserved everything he got," Sandra said, knocking her empty cup off the table and raising her voice.

"It's okay," Officer Wilson said, holding out her hands to calm Sandra. "I appreciate your input, Sandra. You've been a great help."

"Uh huh," Sandra responded, picking up her puffy pink coat and putting it on hastily. She exited the café in a huff as other customers in the coffee shop stared on in bewilderment.

Officer Wilson finished recording the conversation and gathered up her things. She didn't want to stick around after the scene Sandra had caused. She went back to the police station and found Officer Martinez to talk to him about her newfound information.

"That doesn't prove anything," he said, frowning.

"I think she's a compulsive liar. I don't believe she had an affair with Jackson or that she was an extra on the show. She's crazed and delusional. She acted like they were in a serious relationship, but I highly doubt Jackson ever cared about her."

"Ah, but you don't know that for sure, and you have no way of proving they didn't have some sort of relationship. But, even if they did, that doesn't mean she would wait three years, switch the gun on the TV set to kill him, and then kill Clara. Why would she wait that long for revenge?"

"I don't know. I'm sure there's a reason... Anyways, I found these hairs in Jackson and Clara's bed," she said, holding out the Ziploc bag. "They're dark, so they could be Jackson's hair, but I want them sent to the lab for DNA testing before I continue."

"Alright, fine. Wait a minute, when did you find these hairs? Did you go back to the apartment after the investigation?"

Officer Wilson looked him straight in the eyes, not trying to shy away from what she had done. "Yes, I did. I want to find out the truth."

"Officer, you did not have clearance to return to the crime scene after it was closed off. Don't do that again or you will risk losing your job. Do you understand?"

Officer Wilson swallowed nervously, not willing to back down. "I understand."

"Good. I'll take this to forensics and have them verify that it is in fact Jackson's hair and we will get this whole mess sorted out."

"Thank you."

"No need to thank me. I want this case to be closed once and for all."

***

"Sorry to bother you again, but I had to ask you something. You were the best person to talk to about this. Was there an extra on the show named Sandra a few years ago? A woman with curly brown hair who was involved with Jackson?" Officer Wilson asked.

Gus nearly spit out his water and chortled in response. "She was an extra on the show, but as far as I know she and Jackson didn't have a relationship. She was obsessed with him, but he wouldn't give her the time of day."

"Are you sure? I talked with Sandra and she claimed she and Jackson had an affair while he was dating Clara. She said it went on for over five months."

"No, that doesn't sound right. I never even saw them talk while they were on the set. Like I told you before, I didn't know much about Jackson's personal life, but I don't believe he would cheat on Clara. You might want to talk to Edgar about it though. If anyone would know, it would be him."

"Mr. Carver, I have a question to ask you and I don't want you to read too much into it or disclose the question to anyone. Do you understand?"

"Yes…" He said nervously. He was beginning to regret agreeing to the interrogation. Cops made him anxious. They had too much power and often used force when it was unnecessary.

"Do you think Edgar was capable of killing Jackson?"

Gus simply stared at her in disbelief. "Edgar? Why would you ask me that?" He stood hastily, nearly knocking his director's chair over in the process. "Is he a suspect? Do you think he did it?" He asked question after question because he couldn't think straight. No one was safe from being a suspect apparently. He was just happy he hadn't been interrogated as one.

"I am simply trying to cover every possible suspect I can," she explained.

Gus shook his head back and forth rapidly. "There's no possible way Edgar killed him," he said. "The two of them were thicker than thieves."

"Don't you find it a little strange that he was so willing and eager to take over Jackson's role immediately after his death?"

Gus paused, reflecting for a moment. "I thought it was a bit odd. But the more I thought about it, the more sense it made. Celebrities do things like that for friends sometimes. In *The Imaginarium of Doctor Parnassus*, after Heath Ledger died, Johnny Depp, Colin Farrell, and Jude Law took over his role and no one batted an eye. They thought it was sweet and showed how much the other actors cared about Heath and finishing the movie for him. I think it's a similar situation...Edgar wanted to ensure the role was done the way it was intended. Jackson would have wanted his best friend to finish the show and would have been upset if anyone else had taken over."

"Alright. Thank you. This has all been very enlightening."

Gus arched an eyebrow. "Ah. How so?" He asked, curiously.

Officer Wilson realized her mistake. She was being careless with the details she relinquished about the case. "I'm afraid I can't say, but I think this information will prove to be helpful."

"Glad I could help then. This whole thing has been such a shock. I hope you find out who is at fault soon. It would be a shame for them to get away with it. They deserve to be locked up."

"I agree, sir. I'm doing my best to make sure that happens. Is there anything else you can tell me about Jackson?"

"He was a damn fine actor and I don't say that lightly; he could have been great if he had the chance, but that was taken away from him. Look, I don't know who did this or why, all I know is Jackson was not the type of guy who pissed people off regularly."

"It does appear that way…"

Gus scratched the stubble on his chin absentmindedly. "Do you think he had a dirty little secret? Something someone could hold over him and use against him?"

"We may have reason to believe that, but not enough information to know exactly what kind of trouble he was in," Officer Wilson said carefully.

"Was it drugs? So many actors turn to the hardcore stuff when they become well-known. They can't handle the constant attention and scrutiny of being in the spotlight, so they need something to numb themselves. Maybe Jackson did too," Gus hypothesized.

"Maybe," Officer Wilson responded offhandedly. She didn't believe that to be true. There was no evidence of Jackson being addicted to drugs. But she did think there was someone who had every reason to want Jackson dead. It was just a matter of proof as always. Every murderer had a weakness, an exposed part of their armor, some slip-up they didn't consider and left for the police to find. No human was infallible; she just had to prove their part in the deaths and all would be well.

The Long Shadow on the Stage

CHAPTER 38:
Edgar

Edgar retreated into his apartment, becoming more of a hermit than ever before. He had no reason to leave his apartment now. There was nothing left for him in the outside world. His parents hadn't called him after Jackson's death, which proved they didn't care about his wellbeing in the slightest. It was disappointing, although not entirely unexpected. He hadn't heard from them in over two years, after all. But as much as he pretended not to care, it still bothered him that his parents had thrown him out and left him to fend for himself. He had been forced to grow up too fast. It hadn't been fair. He drank bottle after bottle of whiskey, drinking himself into what was now becoming a familiar stupor, throwing the bottles from the couch at random when he was finished with them. He didn't feel the pressure of finding a new acting role, the need to be social and interact with friends and family who loved and cared about him, or the desire to accomplish things and spend his time in a productive manner. Instead, under the influence of alcohol, he was content soaking in his self-loathing. He didn't have to do anything if he didn't want to. He had boarded up the windows of his apartment so no light could sneak in. Edgar didn't need sunlight or warmth or anyone or anything. In fact, the sun annoyed him. It was like a personal affront to his depression. There wasn't even supposed to be this much sunlight in the winter, but there it was, shining through his window, trying to cast a light into his life and remind him that all his brightness was extinguished.

But Edgar was perfectly fine on his own, just as he always had been. Time seemed to pass more quickly like this because he had nowhere to be, no one to bother him or interrupt his well-deserved solitude. The hours sped by in an incredible manner. Sometimes he went entire days without ever moving from the couch, but he was living in a way that he felt suited him, until one day when he was watching TV and realized it was a re-run of an episode he had already seen three or four times. It finally hit him how pathetic he must look. He wasn't living anymore. He was letting Jackson's death destroy him and he realized at last that it wasn't worth it. No person was worth dying over. Because that's what he was doing, slowly killing himself, drinking his years away.

He suddenly wanted to be outside, to feel snowflakes gently kiss his skin as they fell perfectly unsymmetrical, to walk the streets and worry about being mugged or beaten, to live out his dream of being on Broadway, to feel any emotion again, just to feel something. He ran outside without his coat or boots on and fell on his back into the pile of freshly fallen snow. He shivered from the biting cold as snow penetrated his pajamas he had been wearing for at least four days. Quickly, the snow began to soak him thoroughly.

A man walked by on the sidewalk and yelled to him, "Hey, what are you doing down there? Did you fall? Do you need help?"

"No," Edgar responded. "I'm fine down here."

"Okay then. Weirdo," the stranger said, continuing on his way.

Edgar waved his arms and legs back and forth, making a snow angel. He began to laugh hoarsely. His throat suddenly hurt, probably an effect of laying in the snow with no protection from the cold. He laughed until it hurt and lay in the snow, waving his arms and legs in circles, smiling to himself.

The Long Shadow on the Stage

CHAPTER 39:
Edgar

O f course I didn't kill him," Edgar said, astonished.
"We found several hairs on Jackson and Clara's bed, as well
as a blue paracord bracelet, which we sent to the lab for testing and
both came back as a positive match to your DNA."

Edgar hesitated before saying, "I didn't want to talk about this
because it makes me look suspicious, but I suppose I should tell
you now. I spent the night with Clara a few months ago. We were
both having a particularly rough night; it was right after Jackson
died and neither of us wanted to be alone, so I stayed the night at
her apartment and slept in the bed with her."

"You…what?" Officer Wilson asked, her disgust apparent in
her tone of voice.

Edgar stared directly at her. "I know how the situation appears,
Officer, but I can assure you that I had no feelings for Clara other
than friendship. She was my best friend's fiancée. I would never

do that to him. It was a completely innocent night."

"You're clever, I'll give you that." Officer Wilson smiled and shook her head, her curls bouncing as she did so.

"What do you mean?" Edgar asked in apparent confusion.

"You think I don't know, but I'm almost positive. I highly doubt your story is true, but I have no way of proving otherwise. However, your hairs on the pillow are substantial evidence that show you were in the bed, which could easily mean you killed Clara the night you claimed to have innocently stayed over."

"I didn't kill her," he said with conviction. "Why would I do that? She was one of the few people who understood how I felt about Jackson's death. I didn't want her to die! And why would I want Jackson dead? He was my best friend, for God's sakes!" Edgar screamed, spit flying from his mouth.

"You can claim it wasn't your doing as much as you'd like, Mr. Peterson. I've had it figured out for a while now and this little bit of evidence is what I've been searching for. You set up Jackson's death so perfectly. You were the one who bought the bullets and you were even the one to pull the trigger…But you didn't think anyone would suspect you because it was too obvious. Why would Jackson's best friend want to kill him and then frame his fiancée for the murder? It seemed farfetched when I first considered it, but the more I turned it over in my mind, the more sense it made. He owed you hundreds of thousands of dollars, maybe even millions, with no intention of paying you back. He had eaten away at your life's savings. You were losing him to Clara. Once he was married you knew he would be lost forever, too wrapped up with his wife and soon after, children, and a new family. He was the only person you cared about," Officer Wilson said, satisfied with all she had uncovered. "The only part I can't figure out is why you would lend him the money if you didn't want to. That's some kind of friendship to just hand over such a large sum of money."

Edgar smiled at her. "Officer, I can understand how you could reach that conclusion, but I'm afraid your assumption is incorrect. I didn't set up Clara for Jackson's death or kill either of them. I'm not capable of murder," he implored, looking at her with his haunting, almond-shaped brown eyes.

"I don't think you quite understand, Mr. Peterson. *I know what you did.*"

"No, I don't think *you* understand, Officer. Regardless of the truth, I have no intention of spending the rest of my life behind bars. I've worked hard to make a life for myself. I'm too young to waste away before I've accomplished what I've set out to do."

"And what exactly is that, Mr. Peterson?"

"Why, acting, of course. It's always been my dream to be a Broadway star."

Officer Wilson stared hard at him, not budging. "I don't need to hear you admit what you did. The proof of your DNA is already in the lab and entered into the case file. There's nothing you can do now. You won't get away with this," she said, leaning closer to him.

CHAPTER 40:
Edgar

Edgar's hairs which were found in Clara and Jackson's bed were discovered to have been tampered with, so the evidence was thrown out. Since Officer Wilson had been the one to discover the hairs on the pillow and the bracelet in the bedroom and place them in the small plastic bag and bring them in, it was believed that she could have gotten them from Edgar and brought them in on purpose to try to make it seem like Edgar was at the scene of the crime. As if she would go through all that trouble. The police captain thought Officer Wilson was so sure Edgar was the murderer that she was tampering with evidence, which was ridiculous. The surveillance footage had been destroyed. The suicide note didn't match his handwriting when tested. He had truly thought of everything. The worst part was that after her last conversation with him she knew without a doubt in her mind that he had done it, but all the damn evidence didn't prove shit. Not one thing she had found was deemed sufficient evidence and everyone swore it wouldn't hold up in court.

Essentially, none of it had mattered. All her hard work and dedication, her determination to uncover the truth, the evidence they found, the clues, none of it was enough to prove who had committed such atrocious murders. Once the case was officially declared closed, Officer Wilson quit the police force, deciding for herself that she wasn't cut out for the job because she hadn't followed through on making sure justice was served and that the murderer spent the rest of his days in jail. Her worst nightmare had been realized; she was a failure. She shouldn't have tried so hard when it was all futile in the end. No one else was impacted by the case's outcome as strongly as she was and she didn't understand why despite her best efforts, the truth hadn't come to fruition. It was so damn frustrating. She had done everything within the realm of possibility, but it wasn't enough. She had finally done what she had sworn she would never do: give up hope.

Officer Martinez was assigned a new partner, a fresh-faced, young man just out of the police academy. Delia thought he would last a few months if he was lucky. No one could survive Officer Martinez's arrogance. He was notorious for how many partners he had throughout his career. Gus continued to be an asshole, married his third wife, and went on to direct the Anne Hathaway movie, which was a box office success, shattering records globally. He made millions, enough to have the best of everything for the rest of his life. Jackson's parents never fully recovered from their son's death. Susan caught a particularly bad case of pneumonia and couldn't fight it off. She spent weeks in the hospital before dying.

Rick followed shortly after: cause of death, a broken heart. Jessica eventually began to pick up the pieces and start living a normal life again, even after all the loss she had endured. She didn't attend her parents' funerals. She later married and had two children, one of them a boy she named Jackson.

The Long Shadow on the Stage

EPILOGUE

He had done it. He had gotten away with the murders. For a while, he hadn't known if he could pull it off, but now he was free. He was leaving town, moving down south, maybe to Florida, or South Carolina. Somewhere far enough away to be safe. Just in case anyone ever put the pieces together or found enough evidence to prove that everything had been done by his hand. But he didn't think they would, not really, because after all he was the star of his own real murder mystery show.

He drove south, taking back roads the whole way. Yeah, Florida. Or maybe Mexico. Maybe leaving the country was smarter. Mexico was a good place for now. He could always move again if he had to. In fact, it would be nice to be able to travel the world. He could keep moving, never staying in one place for long. He still had thousands saved and when he ran out of that money, well...he would figure something out. He was smart and he had survived on his own for so long. Maybe his parents would miss him when he was gone, but sacrifices had to be made. Or he liked to think they would miss him at least. They would get over it. He had chosen a new profession that required being a loner and that was okay.

When he arrived in Mexico, he would pick a hotel and stay there for a few weeks. No one suspected him besides Officer Wilson. But the case had officially been closed, so he assumed he was fine. There was a possibility that there was a loose end he had forgotten about. He wasn't willing to take any chances. He didn't plan on spending the rest of his life in a jail cell. He wanted to live in this paradise, the warm weather, the ocean, the beach at his fingertips, so many naïve tourists easily manipulated into following him...such easy prey.

But he couldn't think about that right now. His next victim wasn't going to be easy to choose. Before he had killed because he had no other choice, now things were different. He had to pick someone that wouldn't be missed. Or at least someone whose death wouldn't cause a national outcry as Jackson's had.

After Mexico, maybe he would head to the Bahamas. He was sick of the biting cold and relentless ice and snow of New York. Anywhere warm would suffice. He drove through the night, only pulling over at a rest stop once to catch a few hours of much needed sleep. When he woke up, he went to the vending machine to stock up on snacks and soda. He needed the caffeine more than anything. He felt completely drained. Killing did that. At first, he felt invigorated by the loss of life, knowing he had caused it. It felt as if he had been given a new life force, but now it was running dry and he needed to replenish it. He shook his head, trying to clear the thought away. No, *no*. He didn't *want* to kill again. As he pulled his car back onto the road and began driving again, he turned on the radio. The song "Psycho Killer" by Talking Heads was on the radio station he chose. He immediately turned the knob to the next station, anxiety consuming his already agitated state. His car swerved as he took his eyes off the road, trying to find a more suitable radio station. He nearly drove into the next lane where there was oncoming traffic. He pushed the radio's off button forcibly, deciding no music was better than anything he could find. His heart pounded uncomfortably loud in the sudden silence in his car and he wished for something to strike him down and take away his tainted thoughts.

He drove on, knowing he wasn't in the best mind frame to be driving, but he didn't care. All he wanted was to be in Mexico, sitting in a cozy hotel room, staring out of the window at a calming ocean view. He was just so tired…if he only closed his eyes for a minute, he would be okay. He drifted off, relinquishing control, knowing what awaited him if he gave in. He was ready.

Note from the Author

Dear Reader, I would like to thank you for purchasing my book. I hope you enjoyed becoming immersed in my fictional world and that you were on the edge of your seat trying to find out what was going to happen next.

Please consider taking a few minutes to write an honest review for *The Long Shadow on the Stage* on the website where you purchased the book.

The mystery is only beginning and there are still many secrets left to uncover. To stay up to date on news about upcoming releases, as well as receive exclusive content, writing and self-publishing tips, please subscribe to my monthly newsletter on my website www.nicholeheydenburg.com. You can also follow me on Facebook @NicholeHeydenburg, Instagram @nicholehtheauthor, and Twitter @TheWriteWords16.

Thank you and happy reading!

Acknowledgements

Since this is my debut novel, there are a few important people I need to thank for their part in helping me with this accomplishment.

First and foremost, I want to thank my incredible husband, Zed, for all that he has done for me. Without his faith in me, I would never have been able to complete this novel and get it published. His unwavering support and dedication to my happiness are what made me finally realize I just had to sit down and write. Thank you for listening to me talk about my novel for hours and hours the past five years and for helping me work out issues with the plot, as well as figuring out how to masterfully format the interior of this novel. It's because of my husband that this novel exists.

To my wonderful parents, Steve and Michelle LaBarge, thank you both for letting me go to an expensive private college to get a BA in English and for not doubting that I would get a job in my field. I appreciate that you raised me to never let me believe there was something I couldn't do if I worked hard enough.

To my amazing little sister, Kate Postma, I appreciate you always being there for me and for reading everything I've written over the years. You have always been the first one to encourage me to keep writing. You're my number one fan and I can't thank you enough for always cheering me on, even when my writing was terrible.

To my best friend, Alex Noelke, thank you for being there for me every step of this crazy self-publishing journey. I can't thank you enough for editing my novel and giving such helpful feedback and suggestions. I know my novel wouldn't be nearly as great without your help. Also, thank you for the past 10 years of friendship we have shared.

To Alicia Kent, Jessica Skinner, and Heather McKenzie, thank you for being the types of friends who I can always count on, even while being hundreds of miles apart. You always encouraged my writing and believed in me and I appreciate that and your friendship more than words can say.

Printed in Great Britain
by Amazon

45031421R00165